Something Was There

Something Was There

Asham Award-winning Ghost Stories

virago

VIRAGO

First published in Great Britain in 2011 by Virago Press

Introduction Copyright © Lennie Goodings 2011

The moral right of the authors has been asserted.

A CIP catalogue record for this book
is available from the British Library.

ISBN 978-1-84408-683-2

Typeset in Melior by M Rules
Printed and bound in Great Britain by
Clays Ltd, St Ives plc

Papers used by Virago are from well-managed forests
and other responsible sources.

 MIX
Paper from
responsible sources
FSC® C104740

Virago Press
An imprint of
Little, Brown Book Group
100 Victoria Embankment
London EC4Y 0DY

An Hachette UK Company
www.hachette.co.uk

www.virago.co.uk

Contents

Contents

Introduction

Oh, we do love a shivering, spooky ghost story. It is utterly delicious to have the hair on the back of our necks rise in fear and anxiety. And the suspense . . . We know we are about to be surprised, but we don't know from around which corner the dénouement will leap. What will be revealed? What truth was hidden from us? Who will be behind it all? We hold our breath.

We held our breath when we fixed on the theme of Ghost and Gothic for this new collection of Asham short stories, the first published in conjunction with Virago. There has never been a set theme before and we wondered – would we receive stories of the calibre, the range, the excitement that has characterised previous Asham Award-winning collections?

We were wrong to worry. We were overwhelmed with stories by marvellous new writers who took this theme and made it their own.

Introduction

We chose the Ghost and Gothic theme in honour of Sarah Waters, one of our three judges, who has only recently published the wonderful and decidedly unsettling ghostly novel, *The Little Stranger* (from which the title of this book comes). Aside from me, Publisher of Virago, our other judge was Polly Samson, whose brilliant short story collection, *Perfect Lives*, has been wildly praised. So between these two writers with their impressive knowledge, expertise and flair, the entries we received were going to be seriously scrutinised.

Asham received six hundred stories for this competition and shortlisted forty-four of them which were passed to us judges. It was our job to whittle the list down to the twelve stories which you find in this collection and to choose a first, second and third place. It was difficult! We kept shortlisting and reading each other's choices until, over a lunch in Clerkenwell with stories spread across the restaurant table, we hammered out our list.

Is Ghost and Gothic a good female form? Certainly this collection shows that women thrilled to the theme. There is a huge range of emotional responses: here are tales that are poignant, droll, loving and of course puzzling, mysterious and frightening. Some set in London houses, one under an Indian bridge, another in a magical forest. What was especially gratifying was to find subtle, insinuating stories.

I think what did surprise all of us was that our first

prize winner – unanimously chosen – is dryly funny. 'All Over the Place' by Linda McVeigh brings an unexpected twist to a genre that is already taut with the unexpected. We took huge delight in this story. Our second place winner is 'Sam Brown' by Kate Morrison, a chilling tale about young men on the cusp of adulthood at Oxford, and our third is 'The Traveller' by Fiona Law, a beautiful and haunting story about love and mothering. Even though it isn't required, we chose a very worthy Honourable Mention with Gabriella Blandy's 'The Courting', an eerie futuristic story.

It is the tradition of Asham to commission published writers to add to the collection. We are very lucky to be able to include brand-new ghost stories by Naomi Alderman, Kate Clanchy and Polly Samson. And as an extra-special treat – a recently discovered story by Daphne du Maurier.

Huge thanks go to Carole Buchan at Asham and to her sponsors, Much Ado Books of Alfriston, East Sussex; the Booker Prize Foundation and the Garrick Trust. Special thanks to Kate Pullinger who has so nimbly edited the new writers.

I am very proud of this ghostly, gothic group. The best thing I can hope is that it leaves your skin crawling.

Lennie Goodings

Something Was There

Red Branwen

Janet Tchamani

I've got a tale that will freeze the hairs on your balls, sir, if you'll pardon the word. Will you sit, sir? The best chair is the red plush close by the fire. I'll spin it out for you, sir, but stop me please, if I vex you by too much detail. The ladies call me Clappertrap for that my mouth claps up and down so! I was glad to come here, sir. Glad when I heard you wanted a tale and no more. Is it true? It will be a rest for me, sir. Thank you, sir. My name? I beg your pardon, sir. My name's Willa, sir – Willa Jenkins, if you please. I am considered second in this house, Belle Whiley being the first, if you care to know. I know you are from out of town.

It happened two years ago, sir, when I had not long started out in my ... trade. In the summer time, which is odd as I thought ghosts were most at home in the cold, dark weather – winter – Christmas most of all. As I've heard. At least, that was the preference of Mr Charles Dickens and that mad American fellow, Mr Poe, whose tales we all have heard a while since. How sir? Why, it's kind of you to ask. There's a teacher, sir, reads tales to us of a Sunday evening in the gin shop. There's precious few of us bang-tails that can read, you see, sir. Even the labels on our medicines, sir, we have to ask Mr Dutton – that's the teacher I mean, sir – to read to us. I'm one of the lucky ones, having been to Sunday school when I was a girl, though my education was cut short, as you will hear.

More wine, sir? Or a little brandy? Fill your glass, sir. Make free. Shall I go on with my story now, sir? Please be comfortable. Unlace my bodice? Of course, sir, if you wish. You have paid good money for my time.

The weather had been sultry all week, but the storm we expected didn't break. We bang-tails of Eden Place found that pesky inconvenient. You see, sir, we had at that time no place of our own. We kipped down for the night roped together on hard chairs at Ma Coffin's shake-down, leaning against each other's shoulders to sleep, which we did fitfully. It's hard on the older ones – and by 'older' I mean over thirty. It's a tough life when you begin servicing the gentlemen most likely at the tender age of twelve or thirteen. Most that live hard, as we did, don't make it past forty and are glad when dancing days are over. 'A blessed release', Ma Coffin calls it, whenever one of our number turns up dead in a ditch, or an alley-way ... or a gin shop. But I mustn't bore you, sir, with our domestic details.

So, as I say, the weather had been sultry. We were sticking to our dresses like rotten meat to brown paper, we stank of our own sweat and each other's, and our hair hung in greasy ringlets. The horse trough where we normally washed, by the coaching inn, the Four Corners, was reduced to a filthy puddle and we had to make do with a bowl and a rag. When evening came and time to go about our business, we avoided the street lamps, stuck to the shadows. We weren't a pretty sight. Not that the gentlemen who crossed our palms with silver (copper for the older gals) were taking much time to look as they made their choices. You laugh, sir – I am glad to entertain you.

That kind of weather makes them hot under the collar – and at the groin – you see. The younger gentle-men who come in their droves. They come on strong, hard and quick. Thankfully. Unless you've got the 'arther' in your hips or a busted back. In which case you hope for a limp one with muscles like jellied eels ...

Much like my da ... But you don't want to hear about my troubles, sir. They're common to many. 'Tis the lot of women, as they say, to pay for the sins of Eve. And what can we say? We have an answer, sir, but no reason to waste our breath giving it, for they do not listen. Enough to say I was an orphan, fostered by a childless couple, and ran away when I was just shy of my four-teenth birthday. Out the front door in the middle of the night, down to the turnpike. Turned my first trick with the landlord of the turnpike inn for my ticket to London. He was an angel compared to my da. Handled me real gentle, knowing it was my first time, when he could have done anything, with me being so desperate for my escape. An angel, sir, much like yourself. I'm glad of the rest, sir, in this warm parlour. It's rare, sir, for a gentleman to take it easy at an assignation such as this. I thank you, sir. The wine is warming me nicely.

We first noticed Red Branwen standing on the corner under the pie-shop awning where we used to shelter when it rained. We weren't too bothered, to be honest, sir. She wasn't much to look at, pock-marked in the face and shuffling along like an old crone. She was a sorry sight. It was Straw-hair Poll, bless her – you saw her just now as you came in – she that wore the purple gown with the lace collar and smiled at you – who first went over to ask her name and whether she wanted to stand with us for protection. There's safety in numbers, 'specially when the bad men come, sir. Those as use their fists, or worse. Sometimes you get first-timers who are well over the ripe age for the work – widows, beaten wives who've run away from home, you get the picture, sir. They don't last long. We warn them off when we see they have a chance of a better life. The others, we tolerate.

Poll wasn't above a minute talking to the poor soul. 'Says her name's Branwen,' she told us. 'Wants to know if we mind sharing our patch with her for a bit. Says she'll only be here but a day or two ...' Poll put her pretty head to one side and gave us her secretive look. We leaned in close, the smell of our bodies making a sort of womanly fog around our conversation. 'She's a poor, ugly soul: sore, red eyes, carroty red hair, freckles all over her face – at least in all the spots where there ain't no mark of the pox. Shouldn't think she's no competition to us. Leave her be would be my advice, ladies.' We looked at one another and nodded in unison. 'She asked for you, child,' Poll added, turning to me. 'Send the young one to me with your answer, she said. She's taken a shine to you, but be careful – there's sometimes evil in that.'

As I crossed the street and drew near to Red Branwen, as Poll had christened the new arrival, it was as if the sun suddenly drew behind a cloud, though the light was an even dirty-yellow colour from the gas-lamps. I shivered and pulled my old gray shawl tight about my shoulders. She was standing there, still as a statue under the awning, waiting for me, and I caught a flash of her red eyes as she turned her head to me. They went through me like a knife through butter, sir, and I felt the torture of her life, sir, if you get my meaning, though I knew not a thing about her at that time. It was only later that I learned her story ...

'The girls say to tell you welcome and you're not to mind us. Do what you have to, and if you like, you're bid to join us for a glass of gin and a bite of bread and cheese at Ma's after we're done. And if you've nowhere to sleep, you're welcome to an end chair, if you've a farthing on you. What do you say?' I took all my little speech at a rush, still a mite shy, being only fourteen and a mere child to the other women. Red Branwen stared into me with her red eyes for a good while, and then nodded up and down slowly, her eyes never leaving my face. It was uncanny, I can tell you. She smiled as if she knew me. As if she was proud of me. Even then. Of course, now that it's all happened ... Well, I shiver whenever I think of it.

More wine, sir? Thanks. The sofa? Of course, if you wish, sir. Am I lying just as you prefer? Am I shown to advantage? I'm sorry for the holes in my stockings. I shall buy some new with the money you have given me. Red, sir – I always wear red. In memory of that time ...

Well, I worked hard that night we saw Red Branwen. Back and forth to the alley-way I was, for I had promised Poll I would take half her gentlemen, her being with child and all, and her legs swollen and her back aching. Oh yes, sir! We whores have our own peculiar code of honour, you should believe it! Well, my point is I had no time to see how Red Branwen fared. Or who or what she occupied herself with. And the other girls were busy too, with it being so sultry. Only Mags did say she saw her with two different gentlemen, in conversation, and that she was absent from the street from time to time. We never saw her leave, and after that night we never saw her again on the street. She vanished into the night, and no one knew where she came from, or where she went ...

My frock, sir? Of course, if that is your wish. Yes, sir – a red petticoat always. It's my way of remembering, as I said before. Ah! Here comes Mags with our supper! Bless you, my dear. Set it down on the small table and I shall serve this kind gentleman. You look tired, Mags. By all means go to bed. I shall be along when our business here is satisfactorily concluded. Good night, dear, and God bless ...

A good girl, Mags, sir. We have all known one another for a long time and learned to trust ... Would lay down our lives for our crew ... The world may call us scum and other vile names, sir, but we look out for our friends.

Apologies, sir. The tale is past half done. Yes. I remember my last customer that sultry night: a sailor he was, and one of my regulars. He once gave me an ivory bracelet all the way from Africa. He took his time with me, but was straightforward and only wanted the usual. He put his arm about my shoulder as we came out of the alley entrance, so I didn't see at first what was lying there. But then he took away his arm to search in his pocket for coins ... It was a man's corpse, sir, all bloodied, and the hands and tongue and private parts cut off and placed on the belly, like a centre-piece on a dining table. Well, I screamed at first, but when I'd done screaming I began to laugh. It was a strange sight, sir. My sailor put his hand over my mouth, but I bit him hard and let my laughter rip. It was Poll who came in the end and shook me by the shoulders until I became quiet as a lamb and pointed to where it lay.

The girls called for help from the constable, who chased us all off home to Ma Coffin's and we heard no more until next morning, when Ma came to bring us our bread and milk and told us the rest.

You may place your hands where you wish, sir, if it adds to your temporary contentment. And press too – but gently, if you will, or I shall doubtless become inflamed with desire and you shall be deprived of the end of my tale. Yes, a pity – that's right, sir! It would indeed! Yes, sir – that's quite pleasant ...

Ma came in all flustered, slopping the milk from the jug on to the floor in her haste. She sat down heavily on the bench by the door and Mags rushed to take our breakfast from her hands, for they were shaking and we would have gone hungry all day, had she dropped the jug and dish. 'Now, my fine ladies, here's a to-do!' exclaimed Ma, puffing like one of those newfangled steam engines. 'The constables are all over the streets, and you may as well take a holiday, for there'll be none bold enough to come near you until they've taken away the corpses. Five of them – is it possible? And it's a mystery and a horror, and I don't know what! Who could have done such a thing? They say they've sent an officer to fetch Sir Arthur – he who wrote the detective tales – and his friend Dr Bell – who are staying at the Savoy. Perhaps you should go out later, girls, after the lamps go out, for there'll be enough toffs come a-gawping to line all your pockets and mine, for sure! We must spend the day preparing, for you must look your best, all of you!'

Poll soaked a cloth in cold water and applied it to Ma's brow, and Mags fanned her, and I stroked her hand, until she could get her breath. And this is what she told us, sir, in every detail correct and God is my witness. Having examined the first corpse, the Peelers had found a trail of blood on the cobbles, and following it found a second, laid out in the same way as the first. And another trail led behind a warehouse to a gully where a third was found, and another trail from there to the church where lay a fourth, and from there – oh, horrors! – the bloody-handed murderer had laid the victim's entrails, like a long string of sausage to the river, where they discovered a fifth corpse lying on the brink in the same state. All gentlemen, sir, and known to the Eden Place bang-tails as bad men – those with likings, sir, that would interest you, I'm sure, given the pictures in the book you showed me earlier this evening.

Do you feel faint, sir? Has my story troubled you so? I am not sorry for it. We should all take to heart the passing of our fellow creatures, even when they are bad men. I remember their names, sir, and their reputations. George Shells: he that liked a girl to dress as a boy and caused Scottish Hannah to die of haemorrhaging with what he did to her. Franky Blakelock: he carried a whip under his coat and left many a stripe that would not heal without disfigurement. Stephen Maytree: ah, I fell foul of him myself one time – he took the whores up into his carriage, where he had his manservant hold us down while he ... No, that I cannot tell.

Pardon me, sir, but your hands are becoming a little rough. See where you've made a bruise mark on my leg. And here another on my arm. I am sorry to complain, sir, but you know our house rules ... But I am glad my story entertains you.

The fourth was a brute who liked to style himself the Night Lover – we never knew his real name – and he had the worst kind of pox, sir, and knew it, and went with four girls a night for a week, without telling that he had it. It was the death of poor Mary Skinner, for she had no strength in her to bear the cure for it – mercury, sir. And I was with her when she died. A terrible death-bed. A week she was lying there, twisting and vomiting, and crying out for someone to put her out of her pain. At last it was Ma, God rest her soul, who took pity and put the pillow over her face ... Him Poll did see with Red Branwen last, but she had vanished like smoke and was not there to tell what happened.

Ah, those red eyes, sir – and a smell about her like rotten eggs or I know not what! It makes me wonder in so many ways ...

The fifth killed I did not know, but Mags did. Colum McCarthy, an Irishman who worked down at the docks. He was a strange one, and it was he that had his guts laid end to end by the murderer who came amongst us as a scourge that night. McCarthy had a room at the back of the warehouse, for he was manager there. Mags went there one time, and she vowed she never would again. He was a dirty man, sir, who liked to watch a woman perform such acts as no Christian woman should ever have to perform, and he would look, and look, and look. And would be as cold and unmoving as any stone, as if he were watching it done to someone else. And he would keep a bang-tail all night as if he had a monstrous power of self-mastery. And when he had done, at last, he would call his whore a hundred wicked and foul names and push her out the door, flinging his money after her for her to pick up from the ground like a beggar child.

Sir, I have told you before, our house rules forbid any roughness from our gentlemen. I beg you to respect ... Have patience, sir, for you shall have your climax presently. I mean the story, sir. You can laugh? I am glad of it. Laugh now, for we none of us know when our last laugh will come.

So we lay low that day the news came and the streets

were crawling with the constabulary and the blood-thirsty that had come to gape and gossip. We brushed our best gowns and washed and dressed our hair, ready for the evening's business, and there was not one of us that did not dream of the money we should earn, and the treats it would purchase for us girls. Poll swore she would save every penny to keep her babe from the workhouse, though she lost him when he was scarce a month old, and it broke her heart.

Mags had her eye on this house, and had saved a pretty penny already, and the owner, her late husband as he became, was keen to have her in as partner in the business. He was a pimp, sir, as you must know. She inherited it when the gout took him at last, and moved us all in here to safety, thank the Lord. The others had a fancy for new gowns, jewels and other such frippery. And I had vowed to pay Mr Dutton to help me with my reading and writing, and drawing and suchlike, so that I might go for a governess and escape the streets. It was my dream only. I am still here as you see. Oh, you are glad of that, are you, sir? Are you glad?

That night, when I went out, I was looking all the time for Red Branwen, to ask her what she knew of the events of the night before. Had she seen the killer? And was she inclined to tell or to keep it quiet? But then a new customer turned up early – a shy young gentleman who wanted not to be seen, so I took him to the best spot for privacy that I knew. You know it too, sir – the churchyard of St Thomas' by the side of the park. The yew trees are ancient, tall and wide, and the ground under them soft and covered in their needles: a reasonable bed for such as I had planned for the young customer, who blushed as he confessed it was his first time with a woman.

Sir, I insist now that you remove your hands from me, at least until the tale is at an end. You have quite winded me with your squeezings and probings, and I am not so dependent on your lucre that I cannot, if I choose, turn you out of this house. That's a good gentleman. I thank you. I am nearly done.

The night was again warm and sultry, not a breath of wind. I led my young man by the hand till we came under the trees. And there I laid down my cloak and told him in gentle whispers what was expected of him. He took to it easily enough and for once I took some pleasure from the business. But we were interrupted in our transaction, for just as he was preparing to take me again, a group of louts came along by the churchyard fence, shouting and singing and throwing their empty bottles at the gravestones, and my friend was frightened and left me in a hurry. He had paid before entering, and I was relieved for that, but as I rose and adjusted my dress, I noticed that several gravestones nearby had been hit by the missiles of those rowdies, and out of Christian respect I could not leave without at least attempting to remove the pieces of broken beer bottles that desecrated them.

The moonlight was enough to see by, but I had to bend close to the gravestones to be sure of picking up all the pieces, and to rub away the beer stains with the sleeve of my dress. And it was then that I saw it: one gravestone among many, but it was the name, sir, which stood out: Branwen Jenkins, it read. Born in such and such a year, in such and such a place ... But those details would be of little interest to one such as yourself. *Blessed be the woman who righteth wrongs* – the strange inscription. And beneath those lines, another: *Died 1831 at 10, Eden Place in the Parish of St Thomas at the hands of a cruel stranger ...*

I see, sir, that you are suffering from a sudden droop. 'Tis not surprising. Best hide it away, sir, for its use was never part of our bargain. To be sure, I would not be the first woman in my line of business to be short-changed, but here we keep very strict rules, as you must know. However, it is now near midnight, and your time draws to a close. There I was, kneeling before the tombstone, and shivering with a mystery staring me in the face that I was part of, and wondering how close that mystery was to me. Yes, indeed, sir – I see you follow my train of thought. Not only to know that I had been face to face with a dead woman, and in conversation with her not many hours previous, but to see that we shared the name of Jenkins: it brought me to an understanding of horror, more than Mr Poe's stories ever did, and they are truly blood-curdling, are they not? Please sit, sir, and take a little more to drink. Calm yourself, and I will tell you the rest.

Well, I bolted home to Ma Coffin's, and asked her straight out what she knew. She was sweeping up when I ran in all dishevelled, and I took the broom from her and made her sit and tell me all. For Ma sees all, and knows better than anyone the history of the Parish of St Thomas, and of Eden Place, and of generations of bang-tails and their clients.

Ma, bless her always, was loath to spill the truth, even so. For she remembered Branwen, and had been at the house that night, and in the very next room to the one in which Branwen was choked to death – Branwen an old gal who had lasted longer than most and knew many a trick that made them ask for her, in spite of her age, and Ma Coffin a youngster of only eight years, and a 'prentice to the trade, as it were. And Ma knows of the bloodlines that run across the neighbourhood. That the men who had been slaughtered by our vengeful ghost were the descendants of the five men who had paid to have Branwen dance and sing for them that night. How they had each brutally violated her in turn, having broken the terms of their contract with her in their lust, the last having strangled her to silence her loud cries for mercy.

They say Red Branwen was choked so hard that at the last she burst her guts. And perhaps that is why the fourth victim was himself disembowelled, for the wicked, unchristian gentleman who finished her off was no doubt the grandfather of that devil the Night Lover. I cried when Ma told me that, and began to see things differently from before. I felt the vengeful spirit rise within me too, and now it is never quiet.

And then, sir, Ma told me too – for I had to know ... Jenkins is a common enough name, is it not, sir? But I guessed there was a reason why Red Branwen had asked to speak to me in particular, under the pie-shop awning. And the way she had fixed me with those eyes, as if she would draw out my soul ... And then, the red hair and the freckles (though mine are scarcer) – as you see, sir, I look so like her ... I felt something when she was close to me, but knew not what it was at the time ... Ah, this is hard to tell!

You shrink from me, sir, as well you might. And your face has turned pale. And I see you have guessed the rest. Yes, not only are you in the house where Red Branwen lived and died. You are also in the presence of her great-granddaughter, and proud I am of it, to tell the truth. Even though I never knew my family, for as I told you, I was left an orphan. Even though my foster parents hid all from me, the spirit of Red Branwen reached out to me and drew me here from far away ... And now I keep her always in my mind, and keep the traditions of the family. What traditions, do you ask, sir? Well, well, I will come to that. We have made something of a museum of this place, as you see. Yes, indeed. How clever of you, sir! That is why the ladies of this house wear red, and why the upholstery is red, and the wine too … It is a family tradition, and a memorial.

I see you are unable to rise, sir, from your chair, though your face tells me you long to be gone. Your legs will fail you, and the rest will soon follow, and in ten minutes you will be dogs' meat. Your last glass of wine was poisoned, you see. Once I was sure there was no grace in you. That is how we deal with bad men, sir – those who think a contract with a bang-tail no contract at all, and our bodies a mere plaything. I cannot make you out, sir, you are mumbling. Ha! Your last words have been lost forever. The last words of Red Branwen, sir, if you care to hear them, were 'You will pay!' There was boasting in the gin shop afterwards, which made me murderous when I heard of it. They said that was the joke of it: they got away without paying a farthing, and all of them had had their way with her. In a moment you will find your throat become horribly constricted, so that you cannot speak at all. After that, there will be blindness and death. And you may be sure, sir, that when your eyes open once more in the next world, Red Branwen will be there to escort you down to hell fire and an eternity of torment. Which is just what you, and all of your kind, deserve.

The Real Story

Kate Clanchy

To be honest, Giles, I'd like a little more credit and a little less blame. I'd like you, and the directors, and actually, the *whole firm* of Burns Pope Wilde, Literary Agents, to remember how and where this whole story started.

And that's in the slush pile, with me. No, I'm not complaining. I know it's where we all get our start! I'd just like you to recognise, I wasn't so much *in* it, as *on* it. I was sniffing it all over: yup, all of it, the lousy dog memoirs, the saddo comic novels, the picture books by perverts. I was using my nose the way a metal detector uses his bleeper in a prehistoric midden. My nose sniffed out the hand-bound, hand-sewn, loony booklet of *poems*. My nose said, Susannah, hold that one to the light.

Oh, I admit at first I thought I was looking at the world's best quill-pen font. I was peering at the capitalisation, trying to spot the repeats, when I noticed that I was also *reading* the poems. Maybe this guy Ellis Bell actually had something. The landscape, you know? All that death and snow and so forth? I was thinking: Teen Goth; Deep Green; Northern Soul – kinda Now. And then my nose was twitch, twitch, twitching, and I was reaching for my phone.

Of course there wasn't a number, not even a landline. And that's what I mean. Credit me, Giles: I didn't drop the case, I went there. I was on the train to Leeds before I noticed there wasn't a postcode.

Leeds was one thing, you can still shop; Hebden Bridge, also in the Starbucks Belt, nice interiors shops, you'd be surprised – but that place, H_____? What can I tell you? It was off the map. It was off the satnav. Literally: the Tom-Tom screen went blank. 'Them's the Pixels' said the taxi driver, drawing up in the lay-by, waving at a bit of moor. 'We don't go there any more. Not since what happened to Edgar.'

I got out of the car. You know that noise when you're in the country? Those waves in your ears echoing, fading out? Like you've just been unplugged. Well, it gets on my nerves, to be honest, and I didn't know what to do. I'd come so far. I could see a road, though: grey dirt snaking through the grass. 'It's down there, you reckon?' I asked the driver, but he was gone.

Well, I panicked, a bit, obviously. I tried my iPhone: no dice. That place was on – would you call it a ley-line? Like no reception at all? Total cut-off? On the metalled road, you could get anything; I was speaker-camming Cara, getting her to double-check the name on an antique Ordnance Survey. Two steps off it, a total blank. Even my compass utility wouldn't work. I thought about it carefully: I could hike back into Reception, call a cab, or I could walk down that road, into the Beyond. And I took Beyond, and I'd like you guys to ask yourselves, honestly, if you'd have done the same? Really? For a book of *poems*?

I'm not much of an outdoor girl, but I remembered it's important to keep hydrated, especially in extreme con-ditions, so after a mile or so, I stopped and broke out the San Pellegrino. I was in a *dell*, I guess. Sort of a dip, in a sunny bit? There was a stream running down a cliff, maybe six foot high, then it broadened out into a nice kind of brook affair. I mean, I suppose the water had to be polluted – it did foam on the waterfall – but it was clear in the stream. Brown and clear, like beer. So, if you can believe it, I took off my Converses, rolled up my skinnies, waded out to a nice flat stone in the middle, and sat there, cooling my ankles in the flowing Newcastle Brown. I even got out my aviators, popped them on. It all looked better like that, in sepia. More natural.

The water burped and burbled, and I guess there are

birds that sort of gurgle, too, but I know a laugh when I hear one. Something flicked in at the corner of my eye, something white, and I heard it again: a chilly, uppity, intellectually superior, snorty sort of giggle. I took off my glasses and I couldn't see anything. I put them on, and there she was, on the opposite rock. A five-foot figure in a Laura Ashley nightie, crouched on her haunches. Thick dark hair and a grey little goblin face with bushy eyebrows and this horrid, horrid, *quizzical* expression. Like, *what the fuck, townie*, at me and my sunnies.

Well, I didn't run away. (Point for that please!) I said, 'Hi, I'm looking for Ellis Bell?'

'Ellis Bell,' she said, grinning.

'Yes,' I said. 'You see, he sent me some poems—'

'He sent poems!'

'And I've come all the way from London to see about them.'

'From London, to see about them!' she said, and, let me tell you, I had by this time noticed the repeating trick and was just a teensy bit off-put.

'Do you know Ellis Bell's address?' I said, and she stood up on her rock. You could see how thin she was through her nightie thing: muscley little monkey legs, and a horrible dark triangle at the crotch that I'm fairly sure was not a thong. Her feet were bare, gripping the rock like a hobbit.

'Ellis Bell's address,' she said, pointing down the road. I stood on my rock, followed the line of her arm.

I saw a square grey house squatting *Psycho*-like on the horizon.

'There?' I said, quailing.

'Air,' she said, and when I turned, she wasn't there. And yeah, you could write it up as performance art, you can say she's super shy, and she's a fucking genius, but at the time, I was just spooked. Spooked and a little pissed off. I pulled my feet up on to the rock and started to dry them with my socks, and a little flat cloud went across the sun and turned the beauty off like a switch.

'You look like a drain,' I said to the stream, and it giggled at me, smugly. It had those nasty little reeds in it, with like, dirty cotton buds in the tops of them? I'd just noticed them. It took forever to get my socks on, and when I stood up, I couldn't see my way back, only forward, to the grey house, and still the wind blowing through the grass like I was locked in a Wyeth landscape.

'Air, air,' said a voice in my ear, and yeah, I got the fear. I split my Converses on that path. I lost my sunnies. I ran for the *Psycho* house; the black door and the great brass knocker coming into focus like a lifebelt. I battered that door. I hung on to that knocker even when the door opened.

And who opened it? Not a corpse, which I was honestly by that time expecting. Not Her Nightieness, thank fuck, which had also crossed my mind. More Laura Ashley vintage weirdness, though. What I think about *that* is: it's a look, but it's actually quite a demanding one. You need a bit of height, shoulders, cheekbones, and *definitely* the daily Timotei, to carry it off, and the lady in front of me had none of these things. Her head came up, no kidding, to my bra, and her hair was like, *embalmed* into a bun. But at least she smiled at me. Clever grey eyes in a pale little face. She said 'Good day?'

'I'm looking for Ellis Bell,' I said, and she actually clapped.

'You're from the agency!' she said. 'Thank God.'

So there you are, you see. Next time you get started on the 'Susannah got off on the wrong foot with Charlotte' crap (No, you *do*. I've heard you at it), I'd like you to remember that little scene. Tiny, tough white hands, button cuffs, clapping. *Charlotte* clapping.

And what did I do next? Well, lots, actually. Lots of smiling. Lots of chatting. I coped fantastically, I'd say, considering I'd run over a moor and been scared half-witless by a lunatic. I was right in there, going gosh, gosh, what a super place, is that real lime-wash, I love the distressed look on the walls, is it genuine lamp-black? How do you do, Anne, no of course I understand that some people don't talk and prefer to sit by the fire and gibber. Gibbering is my favourite thing too!

Look, I sat right down in their lunatic low-carbon co-op kitchen. I said, super, a real stove! I did not say, omigod, who poured a pan of grease down your weird little sofa and what is that heap of dung on a plate; I sat on the fucker and ate the flaming rock cake. When they pointed at the parlour door and went '*shh shh*', I shushed, like it was really super-normal to be scared stiff of your dad when you're thirty-two. I whispered: and do you write yourself, Charlotte? Poems! Lovely! And Belgium, what a super theme! Could I have a look? Might I take it back to London with me, Charlotte? Oh super, Charlotte, and I'll definitely hire a flaming horse or pigeon or some other fucker to get back to you and let you know what I think of your sweaty recollections of your boarding-school teacher. A fine start with Charlotte. Do you take my point?

Anyway, what was *your* start with Charlotte? I showed you *Professor*. You agreed with me: change the gender, put in a hunky doctor, add, like, a dead nun, and try for the Twilight Mum's market. You didn't say, put her on a retainer, cos otherwise she'll skip off to Hills Wilton with our sage advice in her pocket and that book'll win the Orange Prize and be on *Richard and Judy* too and keep us and one of our better publishers in funds for the next millennium. Or did you? Well, maybe I just didn't hear it.

The next bit, I admit, I didn't do so well. But I was set up. Picture this, okay? No, *feel* this. Put yourself in my ripped Converses, nibble the disgusting rock cakes. You're just about calming down, just about to say to Anne, who has come to sit beside you and is gently and a little spookily fingering your sweatshirt and murmuring about a hard life and something she's been writing and you're just thinking, wow, do we have an abuse memoir here? – when the kitchen door opens and in comes the Goblin of the Moor. You'd scream, right?

Well, I didn't. I just said 'Woo!' Not, you scared the fuck out of me. Or, don't you think you should wear underwear with cheesecloth? Just, like: Woo!

'Woo who!' she said, 'Woo who London!' And she started to dance round the room – like a mime you know? She picked up this rock cake and made like it was a phone, waving it about. 'Reception, reception?' And I'm thinking, I get the feeling you're Ellis Bell, baby, and I'm losing faith in your *oeuvre*, big time. No, that's honest, and I stand by it. You see, when I go looking for writers, I'm looking for the package, not a screwball. You know? I want warm, handsome, presentable, telly-friendly, non-abusive ... I want Patrick Gale. Every time.

Oh really? Well maybe it's a generational thing. Twenty years is a long time in this business, Giles, and like the Internet happened and all the old drunk pervy guys are dead and ... Yes, I agree. This isn't getting us anywhere. Quite. Let's leave it there.

Where was I? Oh yes. Watching the Goblin dancing. Well, Charlotte gets embarrassed and she says:

'Susannah is an agent, Emily. All the way from London.'

'An agent of the devil?' says Emily, still dancing.

'A literary agent,' hisses Charlotte. 'Susannah, this is Ellis Bell.'

'I figured,' I said. 'We actually met.'

Emily flops into an armchair, stares at me, starts picking at her rock cake.

'A literary agent,' she says. 'And what is the book which sets your heart beating, Susannah? What is the literature that raises your doggish hackles?' And she did a little dog mime, *woof, woof . . .*

'Well,' I say, very politely, 'I was awfully interested in Ellis Bell and his poems.'

Emily waves the cake about her head. 'Do you want to bite them?' she says. 'Do they inflame you?' And, no kidding, she runs her hand down her nightie in this really inappropriately sexy way. Anne has her head in her little hands. Charlotte, though, is grinning.

Now, that is the point I fucked up. I know it. If I'd given a different answer, right then, I could have left with the MS of *Wuthering* in my satchel. I'm sure of it. Cos of course Emily's interested in money and fame, really. A certain sort of fame. I think we've seen enough since the Booker to confirm that for us. Oh come on: the *whole* of the *Observer* mag? The photo shoot on the moor? The collaboration with flaming *All Saints*? Do you really call that *Art*? Okay. You do. Art. Should have mentioned it, shouldn't I. Susannah should have said, 'Yes, the poems inflame my heart with the truth of Great Art and make me sweat and salivate,' but, as it happens,

I didn't. I looked at the sneering goblin – yeah, she photographs nicely, but have you noticed, always in profile, mouth shut? No teeth, you heard it here first, – and I said:

'No. But I think you have a great font. Ever thought of developing an app?'

Well, I was out before you could say Man Booker. She sort of clawed me, if you really want to know. And I squealed, and Charlotte and Anne went into this mime of terror cos of the noise, and Daddy and the Door, and – well, I just left. Closed the big black door. Outside, it had clouded over big time. In fact, there was a fog descending; thickest fog I've ever seen, wraiths of it, like dozens of Emilys in hundreds of nighties. I had another go at my compass utility.

Go on then, Giles, rage. Picture the Man Booker pouring through my hands like the fog. And then get over it, please. Because, if you ask me, Emily was looking at self-publishing from the start. She was already self-binding! I think she might even have already hiked over to Hebden before I visited. Hooked up with Claire at CliffTop Books. She was so damn quick off the mark, after all, wasn't she? Had it out a month after *Tenant*?

All right. I can understand you don't want to accept that. But here's another thought for you: maybe, just maybe, *WH* isn't really the eternal masterpiece we're all making out? Maybe it's just a small press novel that got really, really, lucky? You know, warm wind from

Twilight, warmer one from Charlotte, the public in a hot mood for incest, judges all favouring the small presses, Green stuff ensuring the good reviews? In a way, *WH* is very *fashionable* you know? I mean, not as in iPhone, fashionable as in The New Portentousness? Like we live in the urban world and we all feel guilty as fuck so all we want to read about is like moors and stones and pure feelings and all that tosh? And give it the flaming Booker.

Okay, okay, a bit sour. Yup. We'll end it there. But I do want to leave you with this about Charlotte, at least. You've got to understand, Giles, she was always looking beyond the Pixels. She wanted to be where the big shit happened. Look how quickly she'd moved up here. Moving through us was just a part of that: it really was not my fault. Besides, she has a thing for men. The way she fastened on to James at Hills Wilton is actually sort of scary. She wouldn't get *Jane E.* out of her pocket for us, would she? But James just had to dimple, and whoopy-doopy, she reaches in her nasty little hand-sewn under-skirt pocket, and out comes the teen crossover classic. That relationship is *way* over-personal. Honestly. His wife's in fits, and there's nothing she can do, cos it's Charlotte pays the bills. Yup, that's Charlotte. Miss Nicey-Nicey with her rock cakes and her big grey eyes looking over my shoulder.

But I'm sounding bitter. Bitter is not good. Bitter is not my theme of the day. I'm here to accentuate the positive. What I need you, and the firm, to concentrate on now is Anne, and the future. Anne, bless her! It's no exaggeration to say I owe her my life. I was already half a mile off the path when she popped up beside me and took my arm. I was just yards from the boggy bit where Edgar the taxi-driver drowned. I could have been a Seamus Heaney poem, easy as a splish, splash, splosh. As it was, she walked me right out of the Pixels, waited till the cab came, talked me through the whole story.

I gave her my iPhone, she gave me *Tenant*, that day. A nice day's shopping, in any other context. No, come on. *Tenant* got a major Betty Trask. Its sales are more than adequate. And she's segued into Self-Help just seamlessly. AA America is really interested in a tour. And it's Anne, let me remind you, who brought us this. The MS I've got on my desk right now. The one I really want some help with, Giles.

Hot? Giles, it's glowing. It's a rag-to-riches misery memoir that's going to be huge in the states, *plus* a parenting how-to book to outsell *Baby Mozart*. How a boy from an incredibly humble background in Ireland escaped poverty, abuse, and illiteracy to rub shoulders with the careless rich and excitingly pervy in Cambridge University. How he won and lost the love of his life. How he settled in the wilds of North Yorkshire and entered into a unique family experiment. How he raised not one, not two, not three, but four authentic geniuses! (Yup, we are counting Bramwell. Tattoos were only ever a sideline. He's really in demand in Thrash Metal CD covers now. And he's cleaned up. Might even go with Anne on the tour.) Anyway. Just picture it. This is what we're all going to be reading this Christmas. I'm seeing monochrome cover, red indent lettering:

Patrick Brunty: My Story

And a subtitle:

Genius! How you can raise one too!

Because, in the end, Giles, isn't that what we all want to know? Not, I mean, not the high-falutin' stuff. The Emily Romance. The Charlotte Art. No, the real stuff. The stuff we can apply to our actual lives. That's what Anne's got, and Patrick too, once you get past his super-scary nine-foot tall mad-Irish persona. He's the centre of the action remember, up in that house. His was the door that was closed, and now Burns Pope Wilde can open it! I'm seeing serial here Giles, I'm seeing spin-offs, I'm seeing chat-show, I'm seeing *Oprah*. Trust me Giles, it may have taken a few years to get here, but *this* is the real story.

Company

Elizabeth Iddon

This is the kind of storm that floods houses and uproots trees as if they were daisies. We hunch in the dark house and listen to the wind scream along the gutters and down the chimneys. Rain crashes against the empty windows and seeps through the gaps and cracks to stain the dust and cobwebs of years. The house is full of moans and echoes, yet we hear it – a creaking of nails and wood as the battens over the front door are pulled away. As we go to the hall to investigate, the door flies open on a blast of rain and something crawls into the house, down on its belly like a drowning animal.

Josh and I are wary of strangers, of the hurt and change they can bring, but Janie has a soft heart. She sees how weed-wet and exhausted this creature is and draws him in towards our fire, a small glimmer in the vast marble fireplace. She strips him of his sodden clothes and he lies at her feet, a pale and fragile lily.

'Who are you?' asks Janie, but he is beyond answering. We give him tea and bread, but he feeds with difficulty, his bones dancing with cold.

'He'll have to stay tonight,' says Janie. 'It's sheeting down out there.'

It is mere humanity to agree with her. We wrap him in an old sleeping bag, sharp with the sweat of previous owners, and put him as close to the fire as we dare. He is already asleep.

The storm works on us all night. Wind knocks and moans through the old house. Thunder jerks us out of sleep. Lightning photographs our recumbent figures in its quick white light. Over the hours the rain lessens and the wind sobs itself into silence. We all sleep late the next morning.

He is the last to wake. He does not hear feet ringing on the bare floorboards, or voices amplified in empty rooms. We look down upon him, matted hair trailing across his sleeping face.

'He's very weak,' says Janie. 'Maybe he could stay with us for a while?'

Josh shakes his head, a trenchant no. I share his fear. This is a half-man, a nebulous creature, occupying the centre of our space. What if he dies here? What if he lives?

It is not that Josh is our leader, but Janie and I understand his need for safety and the dark past that has made him that way. But Janie also understands how to draw him away from his fear-filled decisions.

She leads him into the next room, to exert her own methods of persuasion. She will twist her skinny legs around him; caress him with her tongue until his reticence melts into a pulse of desire. They will stay there, knotted together on the old mattress, until Janie gets her way.

It is midday before the man opens his eyes. He looks bemused, as if he cannot remember where he is. I move across the room towards him and he gives me a faint smile.

I hardly ever smile these days, but I smile back.

When Josh and Janie return, heavy-limbed and dreamy-eyed, the man is drinking water; all we have.

'Expedition time,' says Josh, although his face is drawn at the thought of it.

He and Janie go off into the town. They will sit, hands outstretched, small vermin in the gleaming malls, hoping for a coin or two to fall before the security men throw them out. Shoppers will ignore them, or curl a lip in distaste, as if they are the scum of existence.

I stay with our guest. He lies in the sleeping bag, warmed now by a shaft of sunlight, and dozes. He does not speak and does not seem to hear when I speak to him. It is as if neither of us is really here.

I do not mind. I was in this house, alone, before Josh and Janie came, although other people have been and gone in the past. It is a Victorian house, with high ceilings, architraves decorated with fruit and leaves, and heavy oak doors that creak when we open them. We only use the ground-floor rooms. The stairway is crumbling and we have used part of the banister for firewood, making it even less safe. There used to be some furniture, but wardrobe, dresser and bureau have been chopped and burned, warmth being more necessary than somewhere to put the meagre things we own. The place is derelict and as long as we slip discreetly in and out under the radar of normal life, no one seems to notice. It suits us perfectly.

Josh and Janie come back from town with bread, chips, and cups of baking hot coffee. Usually they find something in the supermarket skips, or bring buns paid for by begging. Janie must have gone the extra mile for this; not only begged and pleaded, but offered personal extras to some passing predator.

No one says anything about the cost. Attention focuses on the food. Josh's fingerprints stain the virgin bread. There is silence for a long while, as chips and coffee are savoured, comforting against the tongue. There has not been such a good meal in ages. The man eats his share and then sleeps again. When he wakes, I whisper to him:

'What's your name?'

His eyes are fathoms deep, as if they have not seen light in years.

'My name is Paul,' he whispers back.

I have known love and lost it. Up until now that anguish has been better than the ache of wanting someone else. But now that primeval longing is back with a vengeance. I keep close to Paul, making sure of his needs. His health improves, but there is still little life in him. He speaks very little, and often ignores me, yet that distance makes me want him more.

As he grows stronger, he often looks through me and his dead eyes search the confines of the old house or dwell longingly in one place. He is either looking for, or looking at, Janie.

What did I expect? Janie is wafer thin and has a skin of pure alabaster, apart from the razor marks along her arms. Her eyes are lined with kohl, her hair bleached into a tumbled thatch, yet she is intensely beautiful. Her face is contoured by lack of food and although she has little in the way of clothes, she makes them adorn her. She will rip a tee-shirt to reveal the rise of her tiny breasts. A skirt will be shortened to show off her legs; a cardigan cinched in with a tight belt. Lord knows how many times desperate necessities have been bought with Janie's charms. Yet she pays for it with further bar-codes engraved into her flesh. Everyone loves Janie except Janie.

I can see the attraction is becoming mutual. Janie begins to make excuses not to go with Josh into the town. She finds ways of being close to Paul, especially when Josh isn't here. There is a whole ground floor to the house, but she changes clothes and washes herself in front of him, slowly cranking up his desire with a glimpse of neck, leg or breast.

Inevitably, Paul leads her to the mattress. I run to the furthest point in the house, cover my ears and howl into its mouldy corners, but it is no use. Their shrieks of fulfilment drown my cries of anguish. They thrash around in my imagination, happy, lascivious, fulfilled. The pain of it is beyond bearing.

Josh has been unaware. Maybe he has been with Janie so long he takes her for granted. Maybe his miserable existence has locked him into himself so he is unable to see — until he comes back this day, earlier than expected, to a house full of groans. He finds them naked and sticky, transported in their temporary ecstasy, until his long drawn out wail of horror brings them tumbling back to earth.

I think Josh might attack them. His face is rigid, cruel. For an eternal minute he keeps them dangling at the end of his stare, then he closes his eyes and turns away in revulsion. The lovers collapse, a mass of anxious bones.

Things are tense afterwards. Josh leaves the house and does not come back, even when it is time to sleep. Janie and Paul whisper to each other, their faces almost touching. The light of the fire, the meagre food, the looks of love are for them alone. I do not exist.

They sleep together on the mattress overnight, leaving the fire and the sleeping bag to me. By morning it seems as it did before Paul came to us on that rain-angry night. Janie and partner. Me on the outside, the eternal gooseberry.

It surprises me how little Janie seems to care. Josh has phased seamlessly into Paul with hardly a break in the movement of her knowing limbs. It seems as though she just needs a man, a reassurance that she is lovable in spite of her self-hate. I learn to live with this new two-some, in spite of my breaking heart. I have to. I have nowhere else to go.

Then Josh comes back, creeping into the house without any of us knowing. He reaches the top of the collapsed stairwell and attaches a rope to the only bit of banister that is still secure. Before anyone can stop him, he places the looped end around his neck and jumps. Time moves and billows around our screams. Josh's life flies out of him and leaves his body ticking across empty space.

We are used to slipping under the arm of the law. We call the police, because we have to, but none of us is around when they cut Josh down and take him away to an unknown burial.

I am alone again in the house. I wait through moonless nights. I wait through grey days. The floorboards groan as I walk and howl. Eventually, as I hope, a new chill enters the air and a drift of hardly seen particles assembles into the vague form of Josh. He looks lost, frightened by his new amorphous self as he oscillates in and out of vision.

'Who are you?' he mouths, when he sees me in the ATS uniform I was wearing when the bomb fell. When I lost my life, my family and my lover in one searing moment.

'Sylvia,' I whisper back. 'I've been here since the War. It'll be nice to have some real company at last.'

Janie comes back for her few things when it is safe. Paul paces the road outside, afraid to enter. Josh and I stare out at him from the blank windows of the house and he withers into himself, alive with fear. I know he can see me, as he did that first night when he was close to death. Yet he is the real ghost here: the living man who came from nowhere and who has nowhere to go. A man who can hardly state his name.

And Janie? Although she does not seem to care, her conscience is there, gouged deep into her patchwork skin. She has run out of space on her arms and started on her legs. A number of the patches are raw and suppurating. She is even skinnier than I remember. As she collects her few belongings, Josh and I stand beside her, chilling her to the bone, but she cannot see us. It will not be long before she does. Paul will be left alone, friendless in the earthly world. Janie will come back to us, and Josh and I will open our ethereal arms to welcome her.

The Second of November

Celine West

She keeps thinking she can hear people saying her name. She'll be walking down the street, like when she's on her way to work, walking along a pavement busy with people, when she hears 'Estelle'. She hears it from somewhere behind and to one side of her, as though there is someone there who has just caught sight of her and wants her to stop, wants to catch up with her.

The voice is different every time: 'Estelle!' says a ten-year-old girl, 'Estelle' says a fat man, 'Estelle'. At first Estelle always turned, looking expectantly at the other people walking by, ready to see someone she knew. Then she kept moving forward but still flicked her gaze to that blind spot above her left shoulder. Now she has heard someone calling her name so many times that she simply registers it and keeps on walking, she doesn't look.

It is the same when the things in her house move. Estelle and Frank bought the house two years ago: three storeys high, steps up to the blue door, railings, cornicing, picture rails, fireplaces, many bookshelves. Frank has painted every wall inside, in colours called Milk White, Cotton White, Pugin Red.

Almost all of the things in the house are connected to stories that Estelle likes to tell herself, stories about the places they came from and the chain of makers, owners and users. There is a low rush stool with chipped red legs, woven by her mother when she was at middle school. As she sits on it to stroke the cat, Estelle pictures the serious little girl in a green wool skirt, white socks and lace-up shoes, brown hair in bunches, working the thick cords through and up and over with her small hands.

In the kitchen is a large ceramic jug used to store utensils, bought for six euros in a hill town in Catalonia, wrapped in a lurid orange beach towel and cradled by Estelle as she and Frank flew home. Upstairs is a steamer trunk with torn labels from voyages in 1907 stuck on its big black body, with turquoise and gold fabric lining the drawers and hat-boxes inside.

These things are stable. It is the smaller, more intimate things that move. A bracelet she wore was on the chest of drawers, is now on the bedside table. A hairbrush in the bathroom, now on top of the piano. Two ten-pence coins now on top of the fridge.

The Second of November

Estelle spends some minutes staring at whatever thing it is this time, staring at it and swearing it had been elsewhere, saying to herself she knows she hasn't moved it. It is never when Frank is around either so there can be no question of it being him.

Often she comes across something like a pen in the fruit bowl when she has been using the pen upstairs that morning and has been alone in the house since. She looks at the object for long seconds during which she can't pick it up or touch it. At times she thinks of the phrase 'I must be going mad', turning it over in her mind like an unopened box. The sort of thing her mother would say light-heartedly: I must be going mad, I could have sworn that pen was on my desk. At times she thinks, it's a ghost, ha ha. It's a ghost moving things about, to show me that they exist. Ha ha.

Hysterical.

One morning in October Estelle gets up after Frank has left the house. She leaves their bed with its blue duvet thrown back and pillows rumpled. She turns on the radio and opens the curtains; it's cold outside but sunny and the condensation on the old windows makes the light coming into the room soft, watery. She puts a hand to her chest and takes a long deep breath, looking at nothing as she stands in front of the window. When she turns back to face the room the bed that she has just left is made. Neat as a pin, the covers flat, the pillows plumped. Estelle gasps and her hands fly to her mouth as she sucks in air. There isn't, there can't be, any doubt about this. This isn't a coin turning up where you would never leave a coin. This isn't a stupid bracelet that maybe perhaps was left somewhere it shouldn't be by someone when they weren't thinking. This is a bed that was very much unmade, made.

She is cold and her fingertips feel like coins pressed against her dry lips but she continues to stand in front of the window, light behind her, the shadow of her head and shoulders lying on the smooth surface of the bed. She closes her eyes as though when she opens them the last few minutes will be undone and her bed will be warm and smelling of night-time bodies and the covers in a bundle where she left them. Of course this doesn't happen.

'Honey, what's up?' Frank asks frequently now.

Estelle is often silent. Perhaps if she doesn't speak, or move, so often, then she won't be spoken to or find things moving. She no longer thinks lightly of a ghost moving her things around.

'Shall we go away? Huh? How about a holiday? Maybe go to Giles's place, you know, in France? What do you reckon?'

'Sure.'

'Okay. Okay then, yes, let's have a holiday. Not the time of year for weather but hey just to get away, from work, from here, whatever. Something, yes?'

'Yes.'

They fly to Limoges at the end of the month and hire a car at the airport, a silver Citroën smelling of fabric softener. Frank drives for an hour under fat grey clouds, south to the hills of the Massif des Monédières where they have rented their friend's house.

They arrive after some time driving on a small road that winds upwards through fields and autumnal trees. Estelle often feels sick on drives like this. A thickening sensation above her ears and in the back of her throat clears a little as she gulps down the remains of a bottle of water once the car has stopped.

Still she fumbles with the keys dangling from a keyring in the shape of a red cross, her fingers feeling too thick to bend. The click of the lock is the only sound. She goes into the house, in and out of each room like a cat sniffing out new territory with its whiskers twitching.

The main space in the house is part lounge, part kitchen, part empty space. On one wall there is a big stone fireplace with a glass-fronted stove and a dark wooden beam for a mantelpiece, cluttered with burgundy-coloured Moroccan tea glasses. The tiled floor is cold and dirty, flies dead since the summer lie by the bottom of the glass patio doors. The room is echoey; it smells of the dust you find behind radiators.

'Hey sugar, just leave all that and get the kettle on,' says Frank, as Estelle goes back out to the car and starts picking at bags in the boot. He is in and out of the house, turning on the gas, the boiler, the heating. He pats her bottom as he passes her, half ushering her towards the front door beneath its low wooden lintel.

'Make us a cuppa.'

'There are beers.'

'Okay, I'll have a beer then. But don't worry about the bags.'

'I wasn't worrying about them.' She plucks at her long skirt, feeling grimy.

'Whatever. Just go inside, open the beers. I'll get all this in and we can relax for a bit.'

Estelle would rather unpack, would rather bring order to the piles of clothes and books and general holiday accessories that will come spilling out of their opened bags as soon as Frank takes them upstairs. She would rather get their supermarket shopping put away and know what they're having or making for dinner, then sit down with a drink.

Once their things are sorted, Estelle drinks a beer while she makes dinner, filling a large glass dish with pasticcio. She eats while she cooks. She eats bits of the cheese that goes into the white sauce, slivers of tomato from the vegetables, a few – a handful – of pasta shapes, 'to see if they are cooked'. Her skirt wrinkles at the hips and pulls tight round her thighs in a way it didn't in the spring.

The village they are in is so small there isn't even a bread shop. There are just a few streets of terraced houses, mostly stone with steep slate roofs. There is a Place de la Paix with a statue in the centre, a church with chrysanthemums nodding against its walls. Every morning Frank drives the few kilometres to the next village to buy croissants and cheeses and whatever else Estelle has asked for.

On the third night of their stay they have a barbecue in the late October cold, standing in front of the gas flames in big jumpers. A gentle wind ceaselessly moves the large fig tree that stretches above them from the garden next door; that garden is so big that they cannot see the house to which it belongs. Estelle eats sausages, bread rolls, baked potato; she has aubergine slices smoky from the grill, mayonnaise, hamburger.

Nothing has been moved in the French house. That is, none of Estelle's things have been moved. She hasn't heard her name. She has been eating, stuffing herself so there is no room for anything else. It is comforting and sickening at the same time.

'Let's go out for dinner tonight, yes? There was that place on the road into Chamberet, looked nice – the sign said they're open Fridays so we could go there?'

'Sure.'

'Good, sorted. Well I might just read for a bit, we'll go at seven.'

It is the second of November. At the restaurant, in the warm glow of wall lights on wood panelling, Estelle eats chunks of bread dipped in olive oil, pâté and pickles, fat duck, soft vegetables, *île flottante*. A bit of Frank's steak, some chips, baguette, butter. *Petits fours*.

The restaurant is on the edge of a town and it takes them nearly half an hour to drive back to the village. It's very dark on the road but when they reach the village and slow down they see lights in the windows of all the houses they pass. They don't see any people but then they've hardly seen anyone around during their stay; it is nearly winter now.

There are houses on only one side of the narrow road where they're staying. They park the car opposite their house, next to an allotment dotted with tangles of spent plants, garden canes and cloches. Next to their darkened windows the other houses blaze with the light from table lamps and candles, three houses in a row.

'Come on, let's have a peek,' says Frank, slipping his arm around Estelle's waist and tugging her towards the nearest window.

'Don't be silly.'

'Let's have a look – what are they up to, the Frenchies?'

'Nothing, it's just dinner.'

In their neighbours' house the dining table is laid full of food for supper. And in the house next door and the one next to that. But there is no one there. Frank and Estelle stand taking in the sight of the food and, at one table, red wine in glass goblets.

The wind is blowing in the trees as it has been all day.

They go inside and go to bed in the one big bed in the house, under a duvet and a navy blue blanket. It is very dark in their shuttered room.

The church clock chimes through the night, maybe it's this that wakes Estelle. She was in a deep sleep, her body still and heavy, her stomach full. She doesn't know what has woken her but a moment after waking up she hears it.

Softly spoken, 'Estelle.'

She gets out of bed in pyjama trousers and a vest. It's like she's sleep walking. She pulls on a grey cardigan but walks barefoot down the corridor, down the stairs and through the house. She unlocks the front door and walks out into the street, into cold night. Squares of light lie on the road in front of the other houses; the rooms are still lit and tables still laid as when Frank and Estelle stood in front of them earlier.

The doors of the houses are open. Estelle walks silently into the house next door. It is just before midnight on the second of November, the end of All Souls Day, the day to feed the dead, to pacify vengeful ghosts with milk, cakes, plates of stew. Supper is on the table in every house in the village. Estelle pulls out a dining chair and it scrapes on the floor. She sits down and begins to eat.

The Courting

Gabriela Blandy

The first rays of dawn break the darkness above her. The sky separates from the tree-tops, and she blows out the candle as she comes past the Church to Saint Brigid. The lake is dark, an ivy green; thick with salt. It was freshwater some several thousand years ago, until rising sea levels came upon the coast here. Seals have been spotted but, although Macha comes every morning, she has never seen them. The swans are here though. The cob prowls the pontoon and makes great efforts to guard his mate. He is fierce protective.

She removes her cloak and lays it with the linen sheet on the wooden boards at her feet, slipping off her shoes and sitting them neatly beside, coming to the edge of the pontoon when the swans have moved a little further away. The lake is deep and still. She sits and drops herself in, her nightgown riding up. The water is cold, but not like in autumn, when her body cannot fight back and the chill seeps in, diminishing. Her blood holds out and she goes deeper, making the strokes quick and solid, to propel her and work her. She glances at the swans, turning on to her back to look at them that way, making her movements smoother and less likely to splash. The swans watch and then turn, dip their beaks into the water and come back. They are like children playing at mirrors, one a fraction delayed so that she can just make out the leader.

Macha has seen the swans in another performance. It was the pen who led then, on a ferocious sprint through the lake. Her legs were almost out of the water, and both wings were spread, flapping up a splash of foam – quite messy and certainly noisy – until the bird rose, Jesus-like. Not walking, not running, but a ballerina, springing from one leg to the other. Beautiful distances in between. Her wings flapped free and sought to glide, one side dipping and then uprighting to keep the balance. And the cob kept up. He fought for this dance and was just behind, dying down when she was spent, idling beside her, until she started, once more.

Macha had felt the thickness of tears beneath her eyelids, slowing her blinks as she watched and held herself as still as she could. Every cell inside her body rose and lay burning beneath the surface of her skin.

*

The sun is clear of the land now, working upwards. Macha has come out of the water and crouches on the pontoon, drying herself. She rubs the sheet up the back of her neck and into her hair, tipping her head forward and scrubbing her face, thinking of the milking to be done, the butter; until she sees something. She scrambles to the edge of the pontoon and stares hard into the lake, but it is just the water and the rocks beneath, with sea-grass and purple urchins, and then into depth and darkness.

She continues looking – certain of something, though not what. The pen has swum close and stares up at her.

Just when Macha realises the pen is *not* looking at her, she hears the huge flapping, and feels the cob's swoop like a shadow, passing through her. It does. It comes from behind: the power of all that air, pushing at her flesh with nothing, but everything. She cries out and throws herself to the side, grabbing the pontoon. Her feet slip off the edge, into the lake – dragging her so that she hangs half in half out – and there, in the foam and ripples, is the cob's reflection, climbing away. She feels a twist in her shoulder and lets herself go, with the sheet tied about her head. But as she drops she sees into the darkness of the lake and it is changed. Or containing something. It is not how she knows it to be – quite simple and black and still. She kicks with her legs to keep from going too deep. But somehow like that, with her arms flailing and her legs working *hard* and *up*, she is drawn down – like an almighty yank at her ankles – until she hits the rugged bottom, crying out the air in her lungs.

She pushes up as hard as she can and, reaching for the pontoon, leaves the sheet sinking behind her. The swans have flown. They are up the bank on the far side.

She pulls on her cloak and hurries to the house.

Her sister Kelcie is at the door, bringing the eggs in.

It's all right, she says as Macha rushes past. He's not up yet, though you've been an awful long time.

Macha pulls off her wet things and stands close to the fire. She is shivering. Kelcie giggles and wraps a blanket around her, saying: did you forget a sheet?

It's not funny, she says.

What isn't? Kelcie draws back and looks at her.

She wipes her hand across her eyes, rubbing them. Nothing, she says.

I wasn't laughing.

It's all right, she says and Kelcie continues scrubbing, and she lets her body flop in these narrow, delicate arms. She can hear the kettle above the fire, halfway to boil. Her sister's hands are small yet firm. She knows these hands.

Did you ever see something? Macha says.

Kelcie stops. What's that?

See something.

I see you, Kelcie says, shoving her face forward.

Macha pinches her sister's nose. That's not what I meant.

What did you mean then?

She sits down at the table and brings her hands out to hold the sheet on her shoulders and says: that kettle's boiling.

Not yet. Kelcie sits down and gawps at her.

What are you looking at me like that for?

I'm not.

Yes you are!

You're the one talking about seeing things.

I *didn't* see anything, Macha says. I just thought I did. I wanted to know if you ever *thought* you'd seen something.

Lots of times, Kelcie says and jumps up for the kettle.

Macha hangs the blanket and goes into the basket by the dresser.

I've not ironed those yet, Kelcie says.

I can see.

Will you be waking him?

Yes, yes, she says, buttoning her shirt.

She goes up with a tray. Her ankles click on the stairs, stiff in the cold: *tic, tic, tic,* and on the landing she takes smaller steps across the rug. She manages the door handle with the tray balanced on the back of her hand and her fingers straining forward.

A flicker of light dances across the lime-rendered walls as the curtain blows in the open window, dragging in and out. William is turned on his side, facing her. His mouth hangs open.

She drops the tray and her lungs flatten with a hoarse whimper, which arrives from deep down in her belly. She stays like that, staring at him until she hears Kelcie on the stairs calling. Her hands are rolled into fists. The day has changed outside.

Macha? Macha! Did you fall?

Kelcie comes into the room. Oh! she says, and then screams.

Shush!

But Kelcie doesn't. Oh Lord, she says. Oh Lord, oh Lord.

Shush!

Macha steps over to her sister and grips the tops of her arms. Shush, she says, and directs her towards the door, pushing her out into the hall.

She stands looking at the bed, and William. She looks at everything: the faded, fraying rug and the candle on the table; William's silver beard, the hand slipped under the pillow beneath his head.

She sits down on the chair in the corner, hugging her knees.

It is Dr Sheehan who finds her later. He steps forward quickly into the room and then halts at the sight of the broken crockery and catches her on the chair in a ball. He makes a sound, turning to the door.

Kelcie peers around and he ushers her forward, waiting until the sisters have each other in their arms; waiting.

But Macha says: I will stay. And so the two of them stay, clung together while he reaches for her husband's pulse; clearing his throat after a moment.

She comes into the studio and sees his brushes in the jar and thinks, it will be best not to go to the funeral, considering how things were.

She would not expect a stranger at hers.

There is a half-finished canvas on the easel. She takes it down and leans it up against the wall. It is a landscape. There are wild foxgloves and fuchsia bushes; fuchsia bushes everywhere, as they are – a thing that has always amazed her.

It is the path down to the bay, but not the bay itself. They made this walk many times. She always felt he would prefer it that she were not there beside him: for he rarely spoke; and in fact she had to march to keep up. She often wondered why he chose her as a wife, as he stalked away, beneath his wide-brimmed hat, his neck in shadow, both hands like small boulders at his sides. She took one of those hands once, in the first few weeks, having crept up beside him as he paused to observe something further along the headland. He peered down at her as if wondering who she was. She felt a fool, and let his fingers slip from hers and ran down to the bay and then home. Kelcie came soon after that. To be with her.

She crouches down by the painting and squints her eyes, imagining them together on the path.

Marriage had frightened her. Until then, it had been Kelcie and her in their room at home and she thought of nothing else. Not of times that wouldn't be that.

Father took her into the hall one morning, for that was where consultations took place – not in the kitchen; or upstairs. All that was left was the hall. Even in summer. As if the light-dappled shade beneath the mulberry tree was quite wrong for a discussion about marriage.

And that was how William courted her: through Father, in the dark hall.

It had never been a bright space. During the day a misty glow came from the stairs. But not much, because really it was just the top step, and two closed doors: the door to the left, Mother and Father, and on the right, Kelcie and her, sleeping in bunks, till she was seventeen and in the hall, and a week later a wife. She thought that to have her own home would be grand. That to be married to a painter would be grand. She had not thought what it would be about.

As it began, the house was merely walls and doors and it was as if she had always misplaced something: coming into a room and not knowing where to start, whether to sit or stand, or take some other pose and await discovery. And William was often pacing on the other side of the doorway, not able to enter with her in there; she thinking, what does he do? Out there.

For several months she put dinner on the table and called, softly: William? As if he were in the room, right beside her. The word a plea, a soft, *soft* beg, which he would never have heard. If *only* he were right beside her.

Ah, he would say, passing the doorway, looking in to the plates on the table.

He came in and rolled up his sleeves and washed at the bucket. He wiped his hands with the cloth she kept dry by the fire. She knew it would be warm and crisp, that it would almost snap in his palms and crumble over his strong knuckles.

He would sit at the table and she would say: I don't know, it's not bad, but you don't have to eat it if you'd rather not.

He would look at her, but she could tell by his face that he had no idea what to say.

She turns to the brushes on the table and sees Kelcie at the door, looking in.

Will you come and dress? her sister asks.

Macha says: do you think they will expect me to cry?

They will expect you to be on time.

She turns and gestures at the room. I didn't know him at all, she says.

Shush, Kelcie says, stepping forward and taking her hand.

But I didn't. If you hadn't been here I should have died.

It's William that's dead, now come on.

She leads Macha upstairs and leaves her.

The funeral passes beneath a silvery sky, but there is enough light to create gentle shadows on the grass. She watches a cluster of men from the village lower William into the ground, and wonders what he will do in there.

After a while, she steps forward, close to the grave. On the ground, she sees a faint silhouette stretching out from her boot, like another foot beside her, but too thick and black for the muted sun. She cannot move. She knows if she does, the shadow will remain on the ground: it will not move with her. She is too cold to even breathe. Voices murmur behind. There is a pain in her chest, like a thumb pressing harder and harder, and the dim shape on the ground could be her, it *could* be. But she is not sure. She cannot move.

She knows nothing else, but to bring his name into her mind. She feels it there in an awkward sort of way, between her temples, until it becomes a brilliant presence, flowing something down her spine that feels like peace.

William?

And the pressure in her chest weakens, and she can

breathe and the shadow across the ground doesn't move, or flicker, or alter, but she is safe to bring her arm across and drop the earth, rubbing her thumb across her fingertips.

As she steps back, she turns to the forest and knows something, like a thought, but without words. She runs across the graveyard, not thinking of the graves. Or the folk gathered. His family. They call her back, but she continues and slips through a break in the blackberry, and although the skirt of her tunic brushes the thorny branches, it is only their very tips and they have no hold, but to scratch a little.

The ground is soft and green, so green, even in the silver morning where clouds are fringed with charcoal. The strands of grass are wide and thriving. They douse her legs and soon her stockings are wet and cool and her toes slip against each other in her boots. Each tree reaches up high. The narrow trunks are moss-laden and knotted. The vistas between are striped ribbons: first a light green of grass, then darker where spindly low branches have sprouted foliage, up to the silver-grey of sky.

He could be behind one of those tall, straight trunks, she thinks: standing in his hat.

Or over there.

She sees fern, dots of foxglove, lichen-draped boulders ... colours ... green – oh, why did she always press him to speak when all he wanted was to look at the world and paint?

And he never adjusted the fork in her hand and said, Like that, as Father would do: Like that, Macha! Wanting her to be this very specific thing and none other.

No, William would sit with her, in the bay, the two of them side by side on the shingle, surrounded by fuchsia bushes; and he would say nothing. But she would *want* to know. What was he looking at? She would want him to point and say, Can you see, Macha? Because she had not known life without instruction; she had never thought to see for herself. And now she wants to say, Look at me, William, for I am. But he is no longer here. He is gone and she is, and there is nothing to do about that.

William is lying on his back under the bed. His face is grey. He is whistling.

Stop that! she cries, sitting up in bed.

Macha!

She looks across the room in the darkness. The moonlight has cheered the curtains and she can just make out Kelcie's silhouette up against the wall.

Macha!

Yes, I was dreaming. She lies back down, staring up at the ceiling. William was under the bed, whistling.

What was he whistling?

I don't know.

Was he ... was he looking at you?

He was dead. He was in that suit.

Oh God, shhh.

Sorry. It was just a dream. Macha turns over and pulls the rug up high to her ear and says: he wore that suit on our wedding day.

It was the only suit he had.

Yes, she says, and then after a moment: do you think he knew he'd be buried in it?

It was his only suit.

But perhaps he thought he would own *lots* of suits by the time he died.

Perhaps.

I wish I knew.

Knew what?

I wish I knew what he was thinking.

He's thinking how grand heaven is.

No, not *now*. She closes her eyes and draws her knees up close to her chest. I wish I'd known what he was thinking when he was alive.

She climbs out of the bed and goes next door into the room where she had slept with William; some of the time. She stands by the closet, but as she reaches for a dress she stops and feels the blood in her body so thick and hard that she cannot bend. Her lip trembles.

He is behind her.

Sitting on the bed, she thinks. He is sitting on the bed, watching.

And she remembers: he did. He would watch her dress; quietly. His eyes were round not oval. They were rounded by the skin that drooped at each edge, wrinkling down.

He had once sighed and said he wished he was not so old – this was after a long day where he hadn't managed to sketch a thing. She had thought it was because he wanted more time – to work, but it all seems very different now. She had been angry. He tired himself out, running up and down the stairs when there was no need. But now she sees him keeping young in those leaps.

She turns, her breath shuddering. The room is empty. He has sprung out of the window. She knows it. *She knows it.*

She sits on the bed, on William's side, and puts her hand on the mattress. When he slept he breathed in through his nose and out through his mouth so there was always the muffled click of his soft palate. And when she woke and it was silent and she knew he was awake, she would lie fearfully beside him, not knowing what to do, thinking he hated her, thinking, without me he would sleep a thousand sleeps and never be pained.

But now, she brushes his hair back from his forehead in rhythmic strokes until she feels his shoulders sink into the bed, and a great sigh comes from his lungs, with many things riding out into the ether.

Her face is still, her hand on the mattress, stroking back and forth.

She wakes before dawn, to the fresh darkness, the fresh of a new day; not the thick of night. She gets up and has her cloak on the way out. She goes down the stairs and out into the garden. The night is grey with mist, low down to the ground, hovering. The grass is very damp and wets the hem of her nightdress. She walks down to the lake, to the water's edge, and crouches down. It is too black for a reflection; there is only the night. She has never seen this. It is like looking into the mirror and seeing nothing there. But there is something.

It was him. It wasn't a memory. He was standing, waiting for her. He was smiling. He was holding out his hand. And she thinks of how she knew what to cook for him after a time, from him leaving small piles of things on the plate, which he had no taste for; never saying, I don't care for this or that, but in those leavings she grew to know him.

She hurries back home, up the path, and bangs open the kitchen door, rushing through, calling, *William! William!* running up the stairs.

But the room is dark: he is not there as he was. She goes through the house with a candle, whispering into rooms, shining the flame in corners. She goes out into the garden.

William!

Back and forth in front of the house. And then, returning to the lake, crying.

William, William.

Sitting on the shore, weeping. And the day comes up. The candle has blown out.

I saw you, she says. I saw you.

The seeds have blown over from America, she hears him whisper. And she knows he is talking about the fuchsia bushes, for she was always asking how it was they lined the coast so: asking and always sure he was not listening.

All Over the Place

Linda McVeigh

At first, I barely notice the beige lump that's heading my way, and then I realise ... it's me, reflected in the mirrored cladding of an office block. I admit I've never been willowy, but the woman walking towards me is positively squat. It's the type of glass they use, I tell myself, wishing it was true. Geoffrey says I'm cuddly, making me sound softly rounded and desirable, but that's not what comes to my mind right now. I look square and solid. A word my grandmother would use jumps into my head. Stout.

Granny Hamilton could never remember anyone's name. 'The plain one,' she'd say, or 'that buck-toothed girl whose uncle works at the butcher's.' She's been dead since nineteen sixty-two – and I was only a skinny

little girl then – but I know that if she could see me now,
and if she wasn't my granny, she'd describe me as 'that
stout woman – the one with the bald husband'. Isn't it
funny? You hardly think about dead people for years
and years, but when you do the stab of loss comes
straight back to you.

I look at my reflection once more, even though I really
don't want to, and hear Granny's voice again ... 'The
one who looks like she's got a pile of frayed rope on her
head.'

The weather's done that to me. It's cleared up a bit
now, but it was drizzling when I got off the train this
morning and I'd left my brolly at home. That's me all
over. Geoffrey says I'd forget my head if it wasn't
screwed on.

The suit isn't very flattering either. It looked nice
on the hanger in Country Casuals, but I can see now
that oatmeal really isn't my colour. I could perk it up
with a nice scarf, I suppose, but I know I won't. I'll
never wear it again: not now I've seen the horrible
truth. It'll end up hanging in the wardrobe for don-
keys' years, rebuking me every time I look at it. *A
hundred and sixty-five pounds*, it will taunt. *Money
down the drain.*

I look at the pavement. I don't want to see myself any
more. I know what Geoffrey would say. He'd go into one
of his rants about modern architects, saying they all
need shooting, or, better still, being made to live next

door to one of their monstrosities. See how they like it. Bless him. He's the only person I know who actually stops to read those planning notices you find attached to lamp-posts, and he's even written to the relevant authorities once or twice. Somebody has to take a stand, he says, and I agree with him. I mean, who but the young and beautiful wants to be caught unawares in the silvered glass of an office block? It's disconcerting.

I step sideways towards the kerb, but my mirror image doesn't change direction; she just carries on walking towards me, head down, staring at the pavement, swinging her John Lewis carrier bag.

She brushes past me, our shoulders briefly touching. A bit rude, if you ask me.

Seeing your doppelganger on the way into Victoria Station isn't pleasant. It shakes you up. I wasn't feeling all that good in the first place, and this has just put the lid on it. I could do with a cup of tea and a sit down.

I make my way across the concourse towards The Lite Bite, but change my mind about going in when I see *her* inside, stirring sugar into her drink and reading the *Telegraph* with her mouth hanging open. Well, the sugar won't do her any favours, will it? I clap my own mouth shut and sit down outside. There are notices everywhere saying tables are for the exclusive use of patrons, so I choose one that hasn't been cleared yet. If anyone comes out they'll think I've just finished. They should clean up a bit quicker anyway. There are pigeons everywhere. It's not hygienic.

I've just got my breath back when I see her again. She's outside W. H. Smith now, peering up at the departures board with a frown, her eyes all screwed up. Put your glasses on, I mutter. You'll be able to see it then. I wonder how she got over there so quickly. I didn't see her walk past. And then looking behind me into the café, I notice she's still there, engrossed in the newspaper.

I'm definitely feeling peaky now and the sight of cold tea and leftover sausage roll isn't helping, so I decide to stretch my legs, have a bit of a wander before the train gets in. I wouldn't mind a browse through the magazines in Smith's. The new *Good Housekeeping*'s out and it would give me something to read on the train, but, as *she's* standing right outside, I decide against it and go into the shop that sells soap and stuff instead. It's empty inside, but then why would anyone have a sudden urge to buy a fizzy bath bomb before getting on their train?

The shop girls ignore me. Too busy chatting. That's another thing that would rile Geoffrey, but I don't mind. I'm only killing time, after all. I pick up a chocolate massage bar, wondering exactly what you're meant to do with it, and then rub some avocado moisturiser into my hands. *Keep refrigerated*, it says. I couldn't be doing with that. You don't want face cream alongside your lettuce. And then I see myself in the mirror. Or rather I see myself and another myself just behind me, sniffing a bar of vanilla soap. I wipe the sweat from my upper lip. I don't know what's got into me today. I seem to be all over the place.

It's only been half an hour or so, but I feel like I've been in this wretched station for an eternity. It's a relief when my destination finally appears on the departures board. 19.47. Platform 16. Should be home by ten, all going well.

I try to ignore the me that I see eating a croissant at the cappuccino bar at the end of the platform and head straight for the ticket barrier, but I'm already there, fumbling about, trying to feed my ticket into the machine, and then there I am again, on the train, having a nap in Carriage Two and doing some knitting in Carriage Four. I make my way to First Class. That should put her off, unless she's made of money. I can't afford it either, but if the ticket inspector comes around I'll tell him I've been feeling out of sorts and offer to pay the extra. What's the worst that can happen?

When my doppelganger comes and sits down next to me, I sigh loudly, hoping she'll get the hint, but she doesn't. She just sits there, oblivious, rummaging through her handbag looking for God knows what. She gives up eventually, zips up her bag and spends the rest of the journey staring out of the window into the darkness. No sign of a ticket collector, which is just as well really, because by the time we get to Arundel there are four more of me in the carriage and I don't think any of us has a valid ticket.

I call out to Geoffrey as I pull the door shut behind me, but there's no response, so I go through to the kitchen, thinking he'll be there. There's a tuna and cucumber sandwich covered with cling film on the worktop, and two mugs, each with a teabag in the bottom. He's even filled the kettle so it just needs switching on. For some reason, the sight of everything waiting for me like that makes me want to cry. But where's Geoffrey? He always waits up for me if I'm late back. Always. And I could do with a bit of a cuddle and a sympathetic ear after the day I've had.

It all becomes clear when I go upstairs. That temptress has lured him into an early night. I can hardly bring myself to say what she's up to, but Geoffrey's clearly enjoying it. She's doing something I normally reserve for his birthday and other special occasions. I can see the shape of her under the duvet, moving up and down, while Geoffrey lies there with a look of bliss on his face. I stand outside the door until they finish and hear him say, 'Well that was a treat. What brought that on?'

Considering what I've just witnessed I feel remarkably calm. I wander down to the conservatory and look out to the garden, thinking how well the hydrangeas have done this year, and I'm not surprised to see myself out there already, sitting on a patio chair, staring balefully at the moon.

I hear Geoffrey call out to me in the morning.

'You in the bathroom, love?'

He tells me he's going to put the kettle on, but before he can do it there's a knock on the door. I stand close to him as he opens it because he'll need my support. The police officer, who looks absurdly young for this kind of thing, removes his hat and asks if he can come in. I hear Geoffrey tell him he must be mistaken, that I was definitely home last night.

He blushes, bless him. 'I'd nodded off in front of the news,' he says, 'but she woke me up.'

There's an awkward silence for a moment.

Geoffrey stares at the policeman. 'She was definitely here.' But he looks less certain now.

'Why don't you sit down, sir?'

I stand next to his chair and listen to the officer apologising for the delay in informing him, saying there was a problem with making a positive identification because I was a bit of a mess. I watch Geoffrey's face while he listens and I long to help him, to hold him while it all sinks in.

Out in the garden we circle the lawn, wringing our hands. In the hallway we pace back and forward, and in the dining room we stare at the family photos trying to fix each image in our minds.

In the kitchen Granny Hamilton is consoling us, saying we've got ourselves into a bit of a pickle, but we need to pull ourselves together now, and at the front of the house, just next to the police car, we crumple onto the pavement, howling with the pain of it all.

The Happy Valley

Daphne du Maurier

When she first used to see the valley it was in dreams, little odd snatches remembered on waking, and then becoming easily dimmed and lost in the turmoil of the day. She would find herself walking down a path, flanked on either side by tall beech trees, and then the path would narrow to a scrappy muddy footway, tangled and overgrown, with only shrubs about her — rhododendron, azalea, and hydrangea, stretching tentacles across the pathway to imprison her. And then, at the bottom of the valley, there was a clearing in the undergrowth, a carpet of moss and a lazy-running stream. The house, too, would come within her line of vision. A wide window on the ground floor, with a rose creeper climbing to the sill, and she herself standing outside this on a terrace of crazy paving. There was so great a sense of peace in her familiarity with the valley and the house that the dream became one she welcomed and expected; she would wander about the forsaken terrace and lean her cheek against the smooth white surface of the house as though it were part of her life, bound up in her, possessed. It was above all things a place of safety, nothing could harm her here. The dream was a thing precious and beloved, that in its own peculiar individual fashion never unfolded itself, nor told a story, nor followed a sequence. Nor did she remember when the dream had come to her for the first time, but it seemed to have grown with her since her illness, almost as if a stray particle of anaesthetic clung to her sleeping mind like a gentle mist.

During the day the dream would go from her, and weeks or months might pass before it came to her again, and then suddenly in the silent hush of morning when the world is asleep and before the first bird stretches his wings, she would be standing on the terrace before the house in the full warmth of the sun, her face turned to the open window. Her dreaming mind, lost to the world and intensely alive in its own dream planet, would quieten and relax, would murmur in solitude, 'I'm here, I'm happy, I'm home again.'

No more than this and no conclusion; it was a momentary state beyond heaven and earth, suspended in time between two strokes of a clock, and so would be vanished again, and she waking to the familiarity of her own bedroom and the beginning of another day. The clatter of breakfast cups, the street noises, the hum of the sweeper on the back stairs, all the usual homely sounds would bring her back to reality with a shudder and a frustrated sense of loss. Since her illness she had become more than ever absent-minded, so her aunt told her; it was like living with a ghost, with someone who was not there. 'Look up, listen, what are you thinking about?' And she would lift her head with a jerk, startled by the demands made upon her. 'Sorry, I wasn't thinking.'

'You're mooning, always mooning,' came the reply, and she would flush sensitively, easily hurt, but wishing for her aunt's sake she could be brilliant and entertaining. She would pucker her forehead in a frown, and steal up to the old school-room and lean her arms on the window-sill, looking down upon the roofs of houses, glad to be alone yet aware of her loneliness, knowing in a strange unconscious fashion that this was a passage of time; she did not belong here, she was waiting for something that would bring her security and peace like the sunken tangled path in her dream, and the house, and the happy valley.

The first thing he said to her was, 'You aren't hurt, are you? You walked straight into the car. I called out to you and you didn't hear.'

She blinked back at him, wondering why she should

be lying on her back in the road, and remembering sud
denly stepping off the pavement into nothing, and she
said, 'I always forget to look where I am going.'

Then he laughed, and said, 'You silly one,' brushing
the dust from her skirt, while she watched him gravely,
aware, with a little sick sensation, 'this has happened
before.' She turned towards the car and it seemed to her
that she recognised the set of his shoulders and the way
his hair grew at the back of his head. His hands, brown
and capable, they were the hands she knew. Yet her eyes
could not deceive her and she had never seen him
before.

'You look pale and shaken,' he said, 'I'm going to
drive you home: tell me where it is,' and she climbed in
beside him, knowing that the pallor of her face was
nothing to do with the accident nor her recent illness:
she was white from the shock of seeing him, and the
realisation that this was the beginning of things and the
cycle had begun. Then her fragment of knowledge was
gone from her, like the dream that departed at daybreak,
and they were a man and a woman unknown to one
another, talking of trivialities, glad in each other's company. She was telling him, 'It's not very pretty this part
of the world, just suburbs, not real country,' and he
smiled and said, 'All country except the west seems foreign to me and dull; but then I come from Ryeshire.'

'Ryeshire,' she echoed, 'No, I've never been as far as
that,' and she lingered over the word, repeating it, as

though it found response in her heart like a lost chord. 'I've lived here all my life,' she said, and the words trailed away like words belonging to someone else, someone left behind, a younger sister, and she herself wandering through a field of sorrel with the scent of honeysuckle in her nostrils and the sound of a river in her ears, born anew, alive for the first time.

She heard herself saying, 'I remember Ryeshire was coloured yellow in my atlas in school,' and he laughed: 'What a funny thing to remember.' Then again came the flash of knowledge: 'He'll tease me about that one day and I shall look back at this moment.' She must remind herself that they were strangers, none of that had happened, and she was only a girl who had been ill, who was dull, who was absent-minded, and 'Would you like some tea?' she said, formal and polite. 'I think we shall find my aunt at home.'

The patter of conversation, the crunch of toast, the maid coming in to light the lamps, the dog begging for sugar, these were natural, inevitable things; but they held significance, as if they were pictures hanging on a wall and she were a visitor to a gallery inspecting each picture in turn. And later: 'Good-bye,' she said, knowing she would see him again and glad at the thought, but something inside her afraid of the knowledge, wanting to thrust it aside.

That night she saw the valley very clearly; she climbed the path to the house and stood on the terrace outside the open window, and it seemed to her that the old sensation of peace and escape from the world was intermingled now with a new consciousness that the house was no longer empty, it was tenanted, it held a welcome. She tried to reach to the window but the effort was too much for her, her arms fell to her side, the image dissolved, and she was staring with wide-awake eyes at the door of her own bedroom. She was aware that it was still very early, the maids not yet astir, but the telephone was ringing in the hall.

She went downstairs and took off the receiver, and it was his voice. He was saying, 'Please forgive me. I know that it's an impossible hour to ring up, but I've just had the most vivid nightmare that something had happened to you.' He tried to laugh, ashamed of his weakness. 'It was so strong, I can scarcely believe now it isn't true.'

'I'm perfectly all right,' she said, and she laughed back at him. 'I was sleeping very peacefully and feeling happy. Your ringing must have awakened me. What did you think was the matter?'

'I can't explain,' he said, and his voice was puzzled. 'I was certain you had gone away and were never coming back. It was quite definite, you had gone away for good. There was no possible means of getting in touch with you. You had gone away on your own accord.'

'Well, it's not true,' she said, smiling at his distress, 'I'm here, quite safe – but it was nice of you to mind.'

'I want to see you to-day,' he insisted, 'just to make sure that nothing has happened. That you still look the same. You see, it's my fault, if I hadn't knocked you down with the car this wouldn't have happened … That's what I felt, all mixed up in the nightmare. You will let me see you; tell me you will?'

'Yes,' she said. 'Yes, I'd like to see you too,' because it had to happen, she had no choice, and his voice was the echo of her own thoughts, suppressed and unfulfilled.

When they were married, he used to tease her about that first morning after they had met, and how his telephoning had roused her from her sleep. 'You can't escape now,' he said, 'you belong to me and are safe for eternity. My nightmare was indigestion. You must have been in love with me to have answered the telephone so promptly! Look at me, what are you thinking about? Mooning again, always mooning.'

He put his arm round her and kissed the top of her head, and although she clung to him in response there was a little pang in her heart because after all perhaps he had not understood; he would be like the rest of the world, irritated in spite of himself at her abstraction. 'I don't moon,' she said, leaning against his shoulder, aware that she loved him, but part of her still unclaimed, inviolate, that he could not touch, and for all her worship of his hands, his voice, his presence, she wanted to creep away, be silent, be at rest.

They stood at the window of the little inn looking down on the river, the rocking boats, and the distant woods beyond. 'You're happy, aren't you?' he said, 'and Ryeshire is as lovely as you expected, isn't it?'

'Much lovelier,' she told him.

'Better than the yellow corner of your atlas?' he laughed. 'Listen, to-morrow we'll explore, we'll wander over the hills, we'll plunge into the woods.' He spread his map upon the table, he busied himself with plans and a guide of the district. She felt restless, stirred by a strange energy. She wanted to be out, to be walking, not idling here in the little sitting-room. 'Some time I must clean the car and fill up with petrol,' he said, 'stroll up the road and I'll follow later. I won't be long.'

She slipped out of the inn, and up the road to the bend of the river, then down to the beach, stumbling over stones and seaweed and little loose boulders of rock. She came to a creek turning westward, surrounded on either side by trees sloping to the water's edge. There were no boats in this creek; it was silent and still, the quiet broken once by the movement of a fish below the surface casting a ripple on the face of the water. Now the beach vanished into the coming tide and she must force her way through the trees to the high ground above, plunging steadily, excited for no known reason, feeling that the very silence was due to her, and the trees rustled in homage, dark and green, the outposts of enchantment.

Suddenly the path dipped, and she was taken down, down, into the confusion of a valley, her valley, the place where she belonged. The tall beech trees were on either side, and then, as she had always known it, the path dwindling to a mud track, tangled and overgrown, while yonder the house waited, mysterious and hushed, the wide windows alight as though afire with the rays of the setting sun, beautiful, expectant. She knew she was not frightened at the realisation of her dream, it was the embodiment of peace, like the answer to a prayer. At first glance the place had seemed deserted and the house untenanted, but as she came on to the terrace it was as though the white walls flushed somehow and were strengthened, and what she had thought were weeds forcing themselves through the crazy paving were rock plants in bloom. She felt a pang of disappointment that her house should be the dwelling-place of other people. She crept closer, and raising her arms to the sill – always the final action in her dream – she gazed through the window to the room beyond. The room was cool and filled with flowers, the warm sun did not touch the coloured chintzes. It was a gay room, a boy's room, the only formal note the heavy chandelier hanging from the ceiling.

There was a table in the middle with a butterfly net on it, story-books lying on the chairs, and in the corner of the sofa a bow and arrow with a piece of broken string. A jersey was hanging from a hook on the door, and the door was open as though someone had just left the room. She leant with her cheek against the sill, rested and happy, and she was thinking 'I'd like to know the boy who lives here.' As she smiled, idle and content, her eyes fell upon a photograph on the mantelpiece, and she saw that it was a photograph of herself. One that she did not know, with her hair done differently, a likeness which, with all its freshness and modernity, struck her as being in contrast to the room curiously faded and old-fashioned.

'It's a joke,' she thought, bewildered, 'someone knew I was coming and put it there for fun.' Then she saw her husband's pipe on the mantelpiece, the one with the knobbly bowl, and above, the old sporting print that her aunt had given her. The furniture, the pictures, she was intimate with them all, they belonged to her. Yet she knew these things were waiting in packing cases in her aunt's house in Middlesex and they could not be here. She felt nervous and distressed, she knew not why, and 'It's a silly sort of joke,' she thought, 'he is making fun of my dream.' But, puzzled, she hesitated, her husband did not know about the dream. Then she heard a step, and he came into the room. He seemed very tired, as though he had been searching for her a long time, and had come to the house by a different way. He looked strange, too; he had parted his hair and changed his suit.

'What's the matter?' she said, 'how did you get here? Do you know the people who live in the house?' He did not hear her, but sat down on the sofa and picked up a paper. 'Don't pretend any more,' she said, 'look at me, darling, laugh at me, tell me what has happened, what are you doing here?'

He took no notice, and then a manservant came in and began to lay tea on the table in the middle. 'The sun's in my eyes,' said her husband, 'will you pull down the blind?' and the man came forward and jerked at the curtains, staring straight at her without recognition, ignoring her as his master had done, and the curtains were drawn so that she could not see them any more. A moment later she heard the sound of a gong.

She felt very tired suddenly, very weak, as though life were too much for her, too difficult, more than she could ever bear: she wanted to cry, and 'If only I could rest I wouldn't mind,' she thought, 'but it's such a silly joke ... ' and she turned away from the window and looked down the path to the tangled valley below, exquisitely scented, mysterious and deep. There would be moss there, soft bracken, the cool foliage of trees, and the lilting murmur of a brook singing in her ears. She would find a resting place there where they could not tease her, she would crouch there and hide, and presently he would reproach himself for having frightened her, and would come out on to the terrace and call down to her.

As she hesitated at the top of the path, she saw a small boy staring at her from the bushes who had not been there before. His eyes were large and brown like buttons in his face, and there was a large scratch on his cheek. She felt shy, wondering how long he had been watching her. 'Everyone seems to be playing hide-and-seek here,' she said. 'I can't make it out, they pretend they don't see me.'

He smiled, biting his nails. She wanted to touch him; he was dear for no reason; but he was nervous like a startled fawn and edged away. 'Don't be afraid,' she said gently, 'I won't hurt you. I want to go down into the valley, will you come with me?'

She held out her hand, but he backed, shaking his head, red in the face, so she set off alone, with him trotting some distance behind, peering at her, still uncertain of her, still scared. The trees closed in upon them and the shadows, the song of the brook rang near, and she hummed to herself, lighthearted and happy. They came to a clearing in the trees and a bank of moss beside the stream. 'How lovely,' she thought. 'How peaceful, they'll never find me here,' delighted with the mischief she had planned, when the boy's voice, quiet as a whisper, came to her for the first time.

'Take care,' he was saying, 'Take care, you're standing on the grave.'

'What do you mean?' she said, and looked down at her feet, but there was only moss beneath her: the stems of bracken, and the crushed head of a blue hydrangea flower. 'Whose grave?' she said, raising her head. Only he was not there any more: there was no boy, he was gone, and his voice was an echo. She called him: 'Are you hiding? Where are you?' and there was no answer. She ran back along the path to the house, out of the shadows, and she could not find him.

'Come back, don't be frightened; where are you?' she called, and then came once more upon the terrace by the house. With a little sense of fear in her heart she saw that the white walls of the house no longer glowed in the warmth of the sun. There were weeds between the paving, not plants as she had thought. There were no curtains on the window of the room, and the room was empty, the walls unpapered, the floors bare boards.

Only the gaunt chandelier hung from the ceiling, grimy with cobwebs, and a breeze blew through the open window so that it swung very gently like the pendulum of a clock, to and fro, ticking out time. Then she turned and ran fast along the path whence she had come, up and away from the silence and the shadows, running from this place that was unreal, untrue, so desolate, forlorn. Only herself was real, and the great murky ball of the sun setting between the beech-trees at the head of the avenue, hard and red, like a flaming lamp.

He found her wandering up and down the beach by the river, staring before her, crying to herself. 'But what is it, my darling?' he kept saying. 'Did you fall, are you hurt?' She clung to him, clutching the safety of his coat.

'I don't know,' she whispered, 'I don't know. I can't remember. I went for a walk in a wood somewhere, and I forget what happened. I keep feeling I've lost something and I don't know what it is.'

'You silly one,' he said, 'you silly, mooning one, I must look after you better. Stop crying, there's no reason to cry. Come indoors, I've got a surprise for you.'

They went into the inn and he made her sit beside him in the chair. 'I've got a lovely idea, and it's going to thrill you. I've been talking to the landlord of the inn,' he said, his cheek against her hair. 'He tells me there's a property near here for sale, a lovely old manor house, a place after your own heart. Been empty for years, just waiting for people like us. Would you like to live in this part of the world?' She nodded, content once more, smiling up at him, the memory of what had been gone from her.

'Look, I'll show you on the map,' he said, 'here's the house and there's the garden, right in the hollow, running down to the creek. There's a stream about here, and a clearing place in the trees, a place for you, beloved, where you can wander, and rest, and be alone. It's wild and tangled, quite overgrown in parts; they call it the Happy Valley.'

Sam Brown

Kate Morrison

There was nothing in the least sinister about Sam Brown. I can see that now. It was only my own eyes filtering the light wrongly; casting his shape a little warped. There really was nothing about him to make a cat blink: he was perfectly ordinary.

Sam was a thinnish, stooped young man with a roundy face nodding delicately on his long neck, slightly bulging, blue fish-eyes, big healthy teeth and teenage acne scars still shinying up his cheeks. He wore overlarge blue woolly jumpers, ill-fitting blue jeans and brown deck shoes; a standard-issue, middle-class child of academia. A theologian, a choral scholar, a spod, a swot, a keeno. If he'd gone to my school he would have been bullied to bits. It was apparent from the start we were never going to be friends.

Yet it wasn't as though he was one of those truly over developed Cambridge brains who can't even open a door or can only communicate in binary code; whose other faculties (heart, penis) function only as reserve energy sources for the mind. He had friends. He loved music. He was nothing to be afraid of. But I was afraid of him and he was afraid of himself.

The fear of death and the fear of life are very different. The fear of death is animal, primaeval, acute. Our bodies tell us: beware. Something is watching that means you harm.

The fear of life is the fear of our own selves, our limitations and capabilities, and is more like constant pain: a wound in the gut. I was afraid of death; Sam was afraid of life. I believed in ghosts but not the Devil; Sam believed in God but not ghosts.

It was Sam Brown who first played me the 'Offertorium' from the Fauré *Requiem*. The 'Offertorium' in a requiem mass asks for the souls of the faithful dead to be delivered from damnation. *O Domine, Jesu Christe, Rex Gloriae.* Deliver them from the lion's mouth, nor let them fall into darkness, neither the black abyss swallow them up. *Ne cadant in obscurum.* Neither the black abyss.

Fauré's 'Offertorium' starts with unaccompanied alto and tenor voices singing a quiet and melancholy plainchant. The voices and the lines of melody twist around one another like two people praying desperately to themselves, thinking only of their own prayer, as if the harmonies are accidental collisions rather than designed. It makes my body prickle with stars.

No, the only trouble with Sam was the trouble with me too: youth. That was all. At that age, I believed in truth. I thought truth was like a hand moving through sunlight in front of a white wall. We only see the shadow of it, darker or paler as it moves nearer or further away, but the hand exists.

I saw no conflict between this concept and my contempt for anyone who believed in God. I also thought the very fact I had come up with this idea meant I was nearer to the truth than most people. Certainly nearer than Sam, with his little silver fish badge and his essays on the composition of Hell.

It was a shame we were so different, because we had landed as room-mates in the sweetest accommodation in college: a round, fifteenth-century tower room perched a hundred feet up, with an exalted and unparalleled view. You could spit onto a crow's back as it flew below; gargoyles clung leerily on to the stone, tongues splayed out for rain. It served as a prison for recusant students during the Reformation and a young rake sold his soul to the Devil there in the eighteenth century.

When I first saw it I was dizzy to be at Cambridge at all, wheeling my trolley-load of possessions through autumn sunlight with bells ringing all around me and pretty girls bisecting me at right angles across the quad like some blissful Tetris game. The whole place glowed with age, like well-handled wood. The tower was cool and dark as a water-tank apart from one west-facing window that flung its own golden shape across the floor. I wanted to strike the space like a bell, make it ring. I pushed open the window and leaned into the sun over the shocking drop. A flock of pigeons ducked and whirred softly, tumbling beneath me. Before I unpacked anything I rolled myself a joint and lay down in the patch of light, feeling warmth and freedom melt into my bones and watching the window-pane swing gently back and forth in the breeze.

I had never lived anywhere so old, furnished with such dedicated asceticism. Even my little box-room bedroom at Dad's had a telly perched in the corner. The living space contained a sofa, two desks, two wardrobes and a small sink unit. All were spare and upright. No rug warmed the stone floor. The two bedrooms leading off the tower were barely big enough to contain a narrow single bed and a little bedside table; Sam's didn't even have a window. And it was cold as only old stone can be. The very first night of term a hoar-frost crashed in over the Fens from Siberia and scrawled ice on the inside of the window-panes.

It was warm as butter lying in the sunlight with my joint though; even the stone felt soft beneath me. I closed my eyes to savour the heat. When I opened them there was a man squatting on the roof beam above my head, looking down at me. I stayed absolutely still. Even my breath stopped. He was staring at me with hate in his face; a long, spiteful, white face. The rest of his black-clad body merged into the dark roof space, except where his white fingers clutched the wooden beam, tensed to jump down onto me suddenly like a spider. Then he turned his head very slightly away from me, looking down and towards the window.

I couldn't help it; I blinked and then he was gone. Where had he gone? I couldn't move. There he was again; the white face above me. Wildly, I tried to focus on it, but it wasn't quite the same: I couldn't see his eyes; the fingers had gone. I blinked and blinked, my heart kicking out of my chest, forcing my eyes to see what was there: a dangling whiteness in the black with a string above it.

A dead balloon. I sat up. It was a dead balloon hanging from a higher beam, left over from a party. I laughed weakly and went to stub out my joint. After that, the glow of the tower was already a little tarnished for me. Atmosphere is one thing; evil, dangling balloon faces quite another. And then there was Sam.

Sam and I, Samuel Christopher Brown and I, were not destined to be friends. For a start, our names mocked us. Our name-board smirked from the wall at the foot of the spiral stairs: S. Brown and S. C. Brown. Sam Brown and Samuel Christopher Brown. Some bored temp in Admin must have rejoiced at the sight of two Sam Browns looking to share accommodation.

So the Devil finds a way in everywhere. *The Devil my enemy stalketh about as a roaring lion, seeking whom he may devour.* Sam taught me that one too. I went to the college chapel just once, to watch the choir sing Compline. Somebody else took me. I hadn't even realised Sam was a choral scholar till I saw him in his gown, yawking his mouth about like a goose, with the most beautiful tenor voice spilling out from him. *Keep me as the apple of an eye. Hold me under the shadow of thy wings.*

I did try, that first day, when he came through the door into the tower followed by the Brown family unit; all of them fish-eyed and big-toothed. Daddy Brown, Mummy Brown, Sister Brown. I was a little boggle-eyed myself and the room still breathed of marijuana.

'Oh,' said Sam when he saw me, crossly, as if I'd interrupted a family party. 'Who are you?'

'I'm Sam Brown Two,' I said. 'Your room-mate.'

'Oh,' said Sam. Then he turned to his mother. 'Mummy, you have to help me unpack.'

That was it really. I went out and left them to it. After that, we barely saw each other. Sam got up early and was out most of the day; I got up late and was out most of the night. The toilet provided our main point of contact, wedged as it was between our rooms, so we came to know each other by our toilet habits. Sam spent hours in there. Hours. I pictured him trapped between anal retention and expulsion, desperate to push the bastard out but unable to let it go.

It was strange to see so littlo of someone and be so aware of them. I felt his presence like an itch, a scratch, a canker. I knew him by little things like his wet dressing-gown over my dry towel, his mugs piled in the sink, his books on the desk. It was like living with a poltergeist. And he talked in his sleep. It woke me in the night: a continuous low murmur, some kind of communication which sometimes built up to a loud question. Lying there all night, murmuring to himself. Sometimes it broke off abruptly; then I could feel him listening for me. Both of us lying in the dark, listening.

Often when I came in late at night that first week he was still working at his desk: 2am, 3am, 4am, wolf hour, in darkness but for the Anglepoise lamp's white disc on his papers He didn't even look round when I came in. I just walked past and wont straight to bod.

One night, I was sick of it. There he was, still working, the Anglepoise casting his shadow high up on the wall. He didn't look up.

'Hello,' I said. He turned slowly, a little to the side. His head looked big and fragile, poking out on its long stem from his dressing-gown.

'You still on the same essay?' I said.

'I can't finish it,' he said. 'I can't ... I'm having trouble writing.'

'You should take a bloody break,' I said. 'Come to the bar.'

'I can't come to the BAR,' he said, his voice suddenly shouting. 'I can't come to the BAR. I have to finish it. Why can't you SHUT UP. SHUT UP.'

'All right,' I said. 'All right. OK. I'm going to bed anyway. Take it easy.' I set off towards my room.

'Have you heard him?' he asked. I stopped.

'Heard who?'

'The Devil.'

I couldn't help it; I laughed out loud.

'You really need a break. Jesus.'

'That man called him up,' said Sam. He kept tugging hard on the sides of his hair. 'Haven't you heard him? You have to stop your ears. Stop your ears, or he'll get in again.'

'Right,' I said. 'Stop my ears. OK. I'll go and do it right now. Nighty night, Sam.'

He didn't reply. I went and sat in my room, and laughed drunkenly into the pillow till it stopped being funny. Was I rooming with a madman? Oh fuck. I would do something about it tomorrow. I crawled under the duvet with all my clothes on and passed out.

But Sam had got into my head; the tower had got into my head. I dreamed I was in the round living-room by the window, looking out at a magnesium-bright moon. All around me was dark black. I had a helpless, sleepy feeling. I couldn't move. Then a voice right in my ear, low and quiet but precisely audible, said: *Open the door. Open the door*. Even though it said: *door*, I knew it meant: *window*. I was terrified of the voice and struggling to wake up and get away. *Open the door*. I kept struggling and struggling to turn around, to see the speaker and wake up.

When I finally dragged my head round I saw Sam Brown. He was the same Sam; head too big for his neck, bulging eyes, but his teeth were smashed to bits. His mouth was a charnelhouse of stumps, spikes, split and cracked bone and nerve, smiling at me around an O of blackness. I screamed and woke up in a jolt, sitting bolt upright; fear strangling my heart. Had I screamed out loud?

I put out a hand for the light-switch and froze. There was something black standing at the end of the bed.

'I can't sleep,' said Sam Brown. He said it in a low, strange monotone. 'I can't sleep. He keeps talking to me.'

'Get the fuck out of my room!'

'He keeps talking to me. He won't let me sleep.' His voice broke like a child's and he began to cry. 'I have to finish it and he won't let me slee-eep.'

'You're sleeptalking. Sam. Go back to bed!' I kept scrabbling for the switch. The bed creaked and his voice came closer to me.

'Please. Please. Why won't you let me sleep? I have to sleep. Why won't you let me?' He was menacing me, coming towards me; his pleading was disgusting;

threatening. I felt his hand press down on to the mattress by my knees and almost screamed again, just as my fingers found the light-switch.

There was the bed, the door, the floor. Sam Brown with his hand on my mattress, his face crumpled, his lips drawn back from his teeth, his eyes spider-veined with red. He stared at me with no comprehension, gulping.

'I'm not stopping you sleeping, Sam! Get the fuck out of my room!'

For a minute he kept staring at me then he shook his head, stood up again, rubbed his face all over with his hands and looked about him. He was in his blue candlewick dressing-gown. His thin black-haired legs stuck out unappealingly beneath; his hair all on end. He looked like a little boy dragged out of bed by a nightmare.

'I just can't sleep,' he said and sobbed once again, and left the room. As soon as the door closed behind him I jumped out of bed and bolted it. Jesus. Now I couldn't sleep. I lay with the light on, ready to get up and nut him if he broke in, but everything was quiet; not even the low murmuring. He was trying to go to sleep; I was trying to stay awake. I failed.

When I woke properly the next morning I lay in bed for a long time, listening. There was no sound from the tower room. Weak sunlight came in through the blinds. Cautiously, I got out of bed, unbolted my door and peered round. Sam had gone out.

I padded out into the living space, which was always melancholy in the mornings: cool, dim and unkind. I went to the window and leaned on the sill while I ate my breakfast, watching people beetling back and forth in between the grass squares; mist still rising from the melting frost. I wondered what to do about Sam. I thought perhaps I should go and find my tutor and say something to her. I couldn't remember where her office was and it was a Saturday, so I wandered about for a bit and then went to the bar instead. God knows I needed a drink.

In the bar was a small minxy blonde girl who had been flirting with me there the night before. She was well out of my league but it was Freshers' week and she was lonely too, so she flirted. We got very drunk in a big group. She had little black spotted shoes with bows on and she took them off and carried them, which made her even littler. 'I'm so *short*,' she kept saying. 'I'm a bloody Hobbit. I'm a bloody *elf*.'

I don't remember asking them back to the lower room, or how we got up there. I don't think I wanted to go back alone.

To my astonishment, when we did, Sam Brown was already there with a group of people from the choir; all black-gowned. Sam himself was lying on the sofa. There was music on. When we came mumping in drunkenly through the door, Sam roused himself and looked at us.

'SSSSSSSSSSSSSSSSSHHHHHHHHHHHHHHH,' he

said exaggeratedly; furiously, like a five-year-old. 'SSSSSSSSSSSSSSSSSSSSSHHHHHHHHHHHHHHH.' Then he seemed to notice the whisky bottle on his chest. He unscrewed it and took a swig, put the top back on and lay back with his head on the sofa arm; eyes closed.

'Is he OK?' I asked one of the choir people. She laughed.

'Poor old Sam,' she said. 'Such a lightweight. He's OK.'

'He had a really bad night,' I said. She nodded. She was looking at Sam as if she liked him.

'I don't think he's very happy,' she said. She smiled up at me. 'Don't worry. I'll keep an eye on him.'

Someone had looked at Sam Brown as if they liked him. I cast about for my elf-girl and found she had snuggled up next to some other bastard in the corner. Bollocks to that.

I went over to open the window and let some air in. As I fiddled with the latch, Sam Brown wrestled himself up from the sofa again.

'Wait,' he said. 'Wait. Wait. I want to play them this.' He said it in a rush, in the monomaniacal, blind-eyed slur of the fixated drunk. 'I want to play them it.'

He leaned over to the CD-player, prodding at buttons. Then he swung round in a lurch and looked straight at me.

'Listen,' he said to me. 'Listen. You have to listen. Will you listen.'

'Yes, Sam,' I said. 'I'm listening.'

He nodded his head laboriously and lay back down again. I opened the window and leaned out into the night. The stars were out; the Plough swung over me. The first chords of the Fauré *Requiem* sounded: lamenting voices coalescing like mist in a valley and rising. The hairs on the back of my neck stung with cold. I looked down. Something white turned up towards me all that deep, deep way down: somebody's face turned up, looking at me. My eyes blurred with giddiness. Then it turned away again and everything was dark. I snuffed in three great long breaths of night air with the icicle music freezing around me; shivered, and ducked back into the room.

Elf-girl's other beau had gone to the toilet so I sat down next to her on the floor. The music tiptoed into the 'Offertorium', the quiet and desperate prayer. Sam Brown on the sofa was almost writhing to the music; turning his head this way and that and moving his lips. Then somebody passed me a joint and I had some.

I woke curled up on the floor, stiff as hell. Everybody was gone; I was alone. The desk-lamp shone brightly, illuminating its small roundel of desk; everything else was dark. The sofa was empty. It was bitter cold. My mouth tasted of caterpillars.

The CD-player was off; it was dead silent. There were signs of a party still scattered about: the empty whisky bottle, the spilled ashtray, cushions here and there. It was so cold. I wanted to be in my warm bed. I could still hear the notes of the 'Offertorium' processing past me towards the altar.

I tried to move but I couldn't; only my eyes would move. I flicked them about the room desperately, looking for help. Out of the corner of my eye, up among the roof beams, I could see a white oval watching me. I tried to turn my eyes on to it, to distinguish a face or see a string above it. I thought I saw eyes, two dark indentations, but I couldn't turn to see properly. I couldn't even move my jaw to speak. The room was flooded with malevolence; it sang with hate. I flicked my eyes away from the face and saw Sam huddled on the floor near me, rocking back and forth.

'Don't make me,' he was saying, over and over. 'Don't make me, don't make me.'

I flicked my eyes back up to the roof beam. I thought the white thing had sidled closer. I could see the fingers now, clutching the wood; the white face staring, staring, intent as a bird. I tried to speak again.

'Don't make me,' said Sam.

It was a dream. A dream, a dream, a dream. I squeezed my eyes shut, tight, tight; tried to haul myself out of it, back up out of the well, as something scraped on the wood above me.

I woke curled up on the floor, stiff as hell. Everybody was gone; I was alone. The desk-lamp shone brightly, illuminating its small roundel of desk; everything else was dark. The sofa was empty. It was bitter cold. My mouth tasted of caterpillars. Everything was dreadful. Shreds of a dream hung in my mind, white and tattered.

Unsteadily, I stood up, and found myself near to the window with my own pale, wobbling face reflected in the black glass. I squinted at it. There seemed to be another face in the right-hand pane. Then the wind sucked the left-hand pane outward, taking my face with it into the darkness.

The pale face in the other pane was still there. As I watched it faded away, stepping backwards into the room. It made me dizzy. I retched and swayed, tottered away to my bedroom and fell into bed without bolting the door.

The next day, a policeman came and woke me up. They had found Sam Brown at the foot of the tower early that morning. He had fallen from the window, down, down, down, till he hit the stone flags and his head burst and snapped from his delicate neck and his big teeth shattered all across the courtyard.

I didn't tell them about the white face in the roof. I didn't know how to begin. It was bad enough already. Nobody ever said: Murder. The coroner recorded Death by Misadventure after Sam's mother read out a terrible, distressing, unposted letter about his failure to finish his very first essay, his failure to sleep, his failure to make friends, his dreadful dreams, his room-mate's noise and mess and unkindness, begging her to come and take him home because he couldn't do it, he was sorry but he wasn't good enough and he nevor would be, and after a forensic scientist ran through reams of evidence that failed to add up in any conclusive direction and I was sent down from Cambridge for possession of marijuana.

Sam Brown is history now. Both Sam Browns: I changed my name. I am no longer Sam Brown either.

Truth is not the same as fact. Nobody knows the truth of what happened, but everyone knows and the papers all reported one very terrible fact among all the other facts of the case.

This fact, the thing which haunts me more than his death or the white faces watching in that tower to call people into the black abyss, is that after Sam Brown fell into darkness that night, alone and afraid, somebody – something – neatly and tidily, with a vicious finality, closed and latched the window after him.

Vin Rouge

Caroline Price

The village is picturesque and deserted, just as one
imagines French villages, a street of shuttered houses, a
dusty square, a *boulangerie* and bar still closed because
it's not quite three o'clock. How long do they need for
lunch! she exclaims. They're all in bed – he says, and
they look at each other eyes laughing, fingers inter-
twined across the gearbox. They've parked beneath a
lime tree, out of the sun. Not even a dog wanders past.
No one knows where we are, she murmurs, I can't
believe we've done this. But we have, he says quickly,
reassuring, we're here, a whole week to ourselves! –

The *mairie* stands opposite, its dusty flag hanging
limply, there's not a breath of wind. They enter its dark
vestibule together, she clutching the sheet of paper she'd
printed out and translated. Why are you learning

French? her small son had asked, and she'd closed the dictionary with a guilty slam before she'd recovered herself, for mummy's work, she'd reminded him, she's got to go away for a few days hasn't she?

The woman who eventually materialises glances at their paper, *ah oui, le petit gîte . . .* and returns with keys and a string of explanations, did you understand anything? she murmurs as they run back down the steps, no he says and they're gasping with laughter by the time they reach the car.

They've been given a hand-drawn map, she drives while he navigates, go straight over the crossroads, look for a tiny road on the right –

They leave the last house behind, the road is narrow and climbing, rocks and high grassland on either side, *only a mile from the village but you'll feel you're alone in the world* he's quoting, hey it's certainly remote! – as it comes into view, a single stone building where the surfaced road peters out, just a rough grassy track beyond.

The cottage is small but renovated with care, light and airy, an open staircase leading up from sitting room to bedroom, oh I love it she breathes, fresh white walls, a deep window seat overlooking the vast landscape of hills, the bed with its white coverlet and square pillows, come here he says taking her in his arms, I can't believe we've actually done this she whispers again into his chest.

The sun is lower but still hot as they emerge later into the sweet-scented air, nothing, just the grating of crickets, an occasional bird, they gaze round taking the emptiness in, where do you think the track goes to, shall we find out?

They follow the hill's contour for fifty yards and then the path turns abruptly to the right, suddenly there is a noise, listen he says, that sounds like a river – and then, my god! look at that—

Nothing prepared them for this, they're standing on the edge of a gorge, the ground drops away abruptly, a series of rocky projections grown with shrubs and small trees and far below the glint of water, a black thread drawn through the cliffs, it's stupendous! he says. She's pointing, and look! – Ahead of them, several miles down the valley, the fortified town rises from its promontory like something from a fairy-tale, turreted against the sky, what a view of it! it's so romantic – He laughs and pulls her against him, and that's where we're eating tonight –

The following morning they wake late, she kneels on the deep sill to push the shutters back and the room floods with light, the sky's cloudless, it's glorious she calls, we ought to be outside! She leans further, oh look someone else has parked next to your car – A small red vehicle, someone out walking he guesses peering past her, you see we're not totally cut off after all. He pulls her back into the room, you're too tempting, in case they come back! – and she pushes him away laughing, go on, get some croissants from the baker's, I'll put the coffee on –

It's nearly midday when they drive away, we must make an earlier start tomorrow she warns, you know I have work to do! She's here to write about the pilgrims' route, men had travelled through all these towns, climbing hundreds of steps on their knees, I'll help you but I'm not doing that! he's already teased.

The sun beats down all day, by the time they return they are sweat-grimed, exhausted, thank goodness for modern showers! she cries from beneath the steaming cascade. He stands watching her, barred with gold light, you're beautiful he says.

They sleep soundly again, wake together and lie with the same disbelief in each other's arms, you can't tell what time it is he laughs, we should leave the shutters open at night, why don't we, there's nothing around – He gets up to push back the creaking panels, my turn to go to the baker's she begins, I don't believe it! he exclaims, that van's back again – The same one? I think so he says, but how odd we never heard it, well we were asleep she points out.

When she returns with the croissants he's pouring coffee, I had a look through the windows he says, there's nothing inside – He hands her a bowl, it's a *Van Rouge*, don't you like the pun!

She organises their itinerary, takes dozens of photographs, move away she keeps warning, how would I explain your shadow! – They hold hands like teenagers, it's a faultless day, they return home glowing and replete, the solitude is exhilarating, the other vehicle has gone. A dog walker he says, or a mushroom-hunter – Or just an ordinary walker she laughs, we don't know where that track goes to, you might be able to walk all the way to the town—

Much later they drive there to eat, return near midnight, the lane is lit only by the moon, how beautiful it is, let's leave the shutters open tonight they agree, let's go to bed by moonlight.

When they wake the walls are bright with sun, she can hear crickets, raises her head listening, it must be time to get up! – He's already crossing to the window, is that van there again? she calls, had meant it as a joke but he turns without smiling, actually yes, it is.

Outside they walk round it, I just don't understand he repeats why we haven't seen anyone, heard anyone, let's go back down the lane she suggests and see if there's something we've missed –

They follow the track to its sudden bend, again they are standing on the edge of the cliff, the path beyond is thin and faint and then disappears completely. They gaze at each other, maybe she begins there's a way down into the gorge –

They stand as close as they dare, it's hard to see how

he says, it gives me vertigo, just looking down from here. How typically French he adds, stepping back, not to fence it off, or put up some warning signs –

They retrace their steps to the wider track, *ouf!* she breathes relieved, and looks at her watch, we'd better get going, we've got a full day –

I could stay here, he says and she turns surprised, why? To see who comes back to that van – Don't be silly! she exclaims, I've planned so many things – Not you, you go, I'll stay – She stares at him amazed, but we're here together, you can't just sit here on your own all day!

The towns she wants to visit are miles away, they are driving straight into the sun, when they arrive each place is overrun with tourists. Was that worth it? he asks as they pull up outside their cottage again that evening, of course she answers but her voice is strained, you didn't mind did you? He squeezes her thigh, how could I mind, doing anything with you? And at least that van's gone! – Oh forget about that van! she says.

But in the night she wakes abruptly, the bed's empty, as she reaches startled to switch on the light she sees his dark outline against the window, what are you doing? she calls out her voice sharp with apprehension, and he starts and turns back into the room, nothing, I couldn't sleep – Are you watching for the van? she demands, but he shakes his head, no, there's nothing outside – Then come back to bed, please, she pleads.

*

Despite the disturbed night she wakes early, when she checks her watch it's only a quarter to seven, as she tiptoes back from the toilet he opens one eye, it's all right I'm not asleep – She pauses to glance out of the window, well it's back again, maybe that's what woke us both up –

He's thrown the sheets back, is at her shoulder, it's bloody ridiculous he says. Pulling on his shorts and sandals, what are you doing – she asks but he's gone, she hears the front door being unlocked, feels the fresh air draughting up.

The engine's not even warm, he calls when she joins him outside. He's crouching, peering inside, underneath, she watches aghast, what if the owner comes back! As he copies the registration number into his diary, his shoulders set, anger suddenly flushes through her, if this is all you can think about – She turns away, I'm going to the baker's, you can stay here—

But when she returns he's sitting waiting for her at the neatly-laid table, coffee already steaming in two bowls, I'm sorry he says smiling at her ruefully, I just want to know, that's all. She puts the croissants down, you're making me nervous you see she says, I know he admits, I'm sorry, I promise I won't mention it again –

But the van has lodged itself in both their minds, they both know it without acknowledging it, the day runs smoothly but underneath something has subtly changed. For the first time their conversation feels forced, they are both relieved when they return at the end of the day, pull into their place outside the cottage, step out into the utter emptiness. It is she who speaks first, gesturing round, I just can't see what anyone else would come here for! –

He walks a short way up the track and back, it's very odd, there are no signs at all – The ground's so dry she begins, yes he says but you'd expect some marks in the dust at least –

They enter the cottage and it feels different, as if someone's been here in their absence, they're both looking round, she refuses to go upstairs until he has. She sits down on the bed and he sees she has started to cry, what's the matter he asks fearfully, aren't you happy? and she shakes her head, not really she whispers and he goes to stand at the window looking out, so what do we do? Minutes pass, he feels her arms reaching tentatively round him, let's go out, I think I'm hungry that's all –

Later, in the restaurant, she looks at him, takes a deep breath, OK, let's try this. Why don't we sit up tonight, and keep watch. One night without sleep, that doesn't matter, I just want to get this sorted out.

They pile the window seat with pillows, pull a blanket round them, he opens a bottle of wine and fills two glasses. Outside the sky darkens, the moon appears again, the hills are touched with its silvery light. The lane below is shaded in grey, the darker bulk of their car to one side. The quiet is broken every now and then by the call of an owl. He has a torch and a pack of cards, we don't have to look all the time, we'll hear it if it comes, as soon as we see the lights I'll turn the torch off. They play a few hands of whist and then she lays down her cards, I can't concentrate, I don't want anyone to see us, I feel someone might be watching us, I don't want any light.

They sit in the dark drinking wine, time passes, are you sleepy? he murmurs, not at all she says. Very distantly they hear the church bell, two o'clock, three, I didn't realise it chimes through the night – She shivers, he holds her tighter, are you cold? no, are you? no not really, when the weather's so hot it's a relief at night – Their voices hardly audible, why are we whispering! he whispers with a laugh. She shakes her head and shifts her position, glancing out, and he feels her stiffen, but it's there! look! –

The hump of their own car still, opposite, and in front of it another dark shape, I can't believe it! we missed it, we must have been asleep after all! – But I wasn't asleep, I swear it I *swear* it – But we must have been, we'd have heard it, there was no sound – He's gripping her, his fingers hurt, there was no sound, and there were *no lights*, how could anyone drive up here without lights –

She gives a little sob, someone's doing it on purpose, I'm scared – No no, he urges hugging her tightly, it's all right – He's disengaging himself, what are you doing she cries you're not going down are you? I'm— he begins but she interrupts grabbing him, no! screaming under her breath, you're not to go down you're not to – tears running down her cheeks again until he comes back to her, OK OK it's all right I'm here – He holds her, I'm with you, the door's locked, we're safe –

The lane is dark and still, no movement anywhere. For an age they stay there and nothing happens, the owl calls again, the church bells, nothing else. He breathes deeply into her hair to calm his own heartbeats, we'll go and see someone tomorrow, we'll tell them what's happening, find out what's going on –

They return to the *mairie* together, have worked out their phrases, a *Van Rouge* a Citroën he repeats, reading out the registration. The woman takes his piece of paper, they wait for recognition but there's nothing, just a shrug, the same question again, *il y a un problème?* Every day, he says, every morning, but we see no one ... Already thinking how inadequate his clumsy words sound, how banal, they just come across as neurotic and mad, she thinks we're mad he mutters to her in English. She takes over, a red Citroën, she insists, at our *gîte*, do you know who? The woman shrugs again, there are lots of red Citroëns, do they detect a slight sarcasm, it's a very common vehicle in France! She's looking past them, there are other people in the room patiently waiting their turn. Excuse me but if there is no actual problem—

They've no choice but to leave, she's right he admits as soon as they're outside, there are hundreds of Citroën vans she must think we're off our rocker. That's not the point she answers, and then, I think she knew something – What makes you think that? he asks and she shrugs, I just sensed it, my sensitive girl he laughs taking her hand but she pushes him away, walks a few steps in silence and then stops, this isn't working. He follows her, it's impossible when you can't speak the language he begins but she shakes her head, I don't mean that, I mean this, you mean us he is forced to say, yes she says.

His throat constricts, you're tired, we both are, we only slept for a couple of hours last night, come on let's relax today let's do something nice – Speaking calmly until she nods her head, let's make the most of these last two days he urges, don't feel under pressure, I don't want to put any pressure on you –

They drive through the hills for miles, there's a lake on the map and a restaurant overlooking it, paths through the trees and beaches where men are fishing, it's a normal Thursday afternoon. And they return dazed with sun and alcohol, everything seems distant, the red van has gone, they enter the quiet of their cottage and climb the stairs, fall separately onto the bed, did you lock the door? she remembers eyes closed and hardly hears him answer yes.

The window is open, they surface again to faint

chimes, seven eight nine ... He lifts his head, counting, it's late but it doesn't matter, everywhere's open late – I don't know whether I'm hungry she murmurs dully, we ought to eat something he says, let's have a quick shower and find a *crêperie*, somewhere simple like that –

While she's in the bathroom he goes back outside, walks over to their car, gazes at the lane on either side. On an impulse he picks some long thin twigs from the bank, has just thought of this, and lays them across the road, they are thin and brittle, break under the slightest pressure. There's no wind to disturb them. He scatters more over the ground where the red van always parks.

The evening disintegrates into argument, he's annoyed at himself for being drawn into laying a trap, she makes a point of not mentioning the van at all but criticises everything else, they end up sitting in silence like two strangers. When they return, much later, he can't stop himself from checking the ground, surreptitiously, before he switches off the headlights, yes they are still in place, and he follows her angrily inside.

Upstairs they finish one bottle of wine and he goes back down for another, let's get smashed, at least we'll sleep ... She looks at him sadly, her words slurred with drink, I suppose it was always going to end like this ... and he throws his glass suddenly against the wall, it was empty but a few red drops splash over the plaster, fragments of glass tinkle onto the floor. Bloody hell bloody hell he mutters as he scrubs and sweeps and behind him from the bed he hears her laugh, a cold little laugh that he doesn't recognise.

They sleep fitfully, each time they re-enter consciousness they listen but hear nothing, there is no other light but the moon's, it is exactly as it has been each night. And as it has been each night, the red van is there again, back in its place outside.

They wake finally feeling terrible, it's still early but they need to get up, clear their heads. She studiedly ignores the Citroën but her hands are trembling as she opens the front door, I'm going to the baker's she says without looking at him, I'm not taking the car, I need the air. Do you want me to come with you? he asks, no she says shaking her head.

He watches her disappear into the still hazy distance and a furious despair fills his throat, he turns and thumps his fist against the door-frame and feels the scalding in his eyes. A few insects are hovering over the grass, a raptor screams somewhere. The sun is already gathering its warmth. He looks over at his car, and the red van parked beyond it, and then walks slowly over to them.

The sticks are where he'd laid them, untouched, unbroken. The Citroën has driven over them without making a mark.

Fear and fury make him tremble. He kicks the van, thumps its bonnet, tugs at the door handles, and the door on the driver's side opens, nearly making him fall. The interior smells faintly of cigarettes, the tank is still half full. They've taken the key but when he releases the handbrake the car rolls forward, he pushes harder, it's not heavy, he's able to set it rolling quite fast. With one hand on the wheel and the other on the door-frame he runs with it, it picks up speed quickly, the momentum it gathers takes them both down the grassy track, it bumps forward easily over the stones and tussocks still gathering speed, when they reach the bend he turns with it and it runs downwards towards the edge of the ravine, he couldn't stop it now if he wanted to. At the last moment he lets go, jumps back, stands there shaking a little as the front wheels go over, as it teeters for a moment suspended over the rock face and then tips forward, he steps nearer to watch, the terrible fascination of seeing it turning and turning branches breaking in its path rocks dislodged and the sound of cracking and breaking and then a sound almost like a human scream and in the window a reflection that could almost have been arms flailing.

She's halfway back from the village when she sees him coming towards her, neither of them are walking quickly and they don't alter their speed. When they meet they say nothing at first and don't look at each other but he turns to walk by her side and hears her draw a deep breath, well you find out things when you walk, there's a house just before you get to the village, there was a woman in the garden, a Dutch woman who lives here, I've found out something unpleasant about our *gîte* –

The red van's gone, he says, and feels her look at him, gone? yes, it's gone he repeats, without slowing his pace. Did you see—? she begins, no he says, it was there and when I next looked it had gone.

They walk on, after a moment he hears her voice again, dry and brittle, don't you want to know what she said, she was in the *mairie* when we went in yesterday, she overheard us say we were staying in the *gîte* –

No he mutters but she carries on stiffly, determined, she told me about the man who used to live there years ago, it was his house, he was besotted by some local woman. She told him she was leaving him to go back to her husband and he was so distraught he drove them both over the edge of the cliff—

Her voice, devoid of emotion, hangs in the air. Their footsteps on the road surface are the only human sounds. A pair of large brown butterflies dance across in front of them, a lizard rustles away, or maybe it's a snake. Very far above, and silently, an aeroplane crosses the immense sky. As the road dips downwards the solid square of their cottage comes into view, isolated, peaceful. No one wanted to buy it, afterwards, she continues. So the Commune bought it, and decided to rent it out as a *gîte*— She stops again, shielding her eyes with one hand, and points. I thought you said that the red van had gone.

The Traveller

Fiona Law

Looking down through scrawny beech branches, I watch
the traveller walk along the remote path tracing the edge
of the woods. He has no idea I am here. To his left are
the grassy hills, to his right the woods; no inn, no hut,
not a dwelling place in sight. Fallen leaves scuttle up
behind him, harried by the breeze. He glances back,
footsteps faltering and I will him to break his journey,
drawing him to rest. As if in response his pace slackens,
he regards the apricot tinge seeping into the clouds
strewn across a watery sky. Yes! The traveller veers off
the road and crosses to the trees.

He drops his gear in the shade of a yew where the
ground is smooth and bare, while I loiter nearby in the
rim of the woods. Soon he has a fine fire going – hot

enough to cook on and dry his cloak and later it will keep the dark and the beasts at bay.

With hardly an inkling of my presence, he sips a brew and stares pensively into the flames. Tired. He is weary of travel and from the direction of his approach I know he is homeward bound. See, as I watch him I learn about him. I know he has come a long way for the tattoos on his hands, snaking up his arms, show me that he hails from the *cors* further inland.

We call them 'bog people' and we are not overly friendly with them. When we happen to cross paths with these bog people we trade a bit or squabble, and we have had the occasional bloody clash. My mother once told me her mother's cousin married one of the bog people. She left her own clan on the woodland coast and went to live with him on the *cors*.

I drift down, slowly closing in on the traveller. From a young oak, whose dying leaves still cling on, I watch as he spreads out his bedroll. He busies himself, rummages in his gear. The sun has trailed the last of his golden slants along the fields and up brambles and trees and now affords only a dull blue hue, which hovers. Long shadows swell and deepen across field and track, and the woodland sucks them in, growing darker sooner. The damp creeps up from under the mulch, anticipating the night with glee.

I move from tree to tree like air, a trail of amber leaves drifting down in my wake, and I alight on lower boughs.

My presence disturbs the sparrows and sets them twittering in their nests as they settle.

Unlike the birds, this traveller will not bed down at the end of the day. Does he grow aware of me, I wonder? For he seems restless, casting about in the dusk for something to do. His eyes have a resolute focus as he searches. So intense are they that, as he pulls a hatchet out of his gear, I believe he has seen me.

But he moves past. I breathe a sigh, a faint zephyr, and more leaves fall and I drop with them to the ground. I press myself against the trunk of a tree and watch.

No, he still does not sense me, this man. He examines the oak I hid in, fingering the bark of a low branch, then he moves on to a holly and quickly on to another oak. I see he is mature but not old. Although his long hair is thinning, greying at the temples, he moves with graceful agility. But he will not venture too deeply into the woods. His steps bring him back to the yew, where his fire burns. He stands, legs astride, regarding the yew, running graceful fingers along rippling, fibrous branches.

Stretching his slim frame, reaching higher, he finds where the end of a branch has snapped off. Although leafless now, the wood still lives. He brings his hatchet back and swipes, one clean blow. I reel with the memories that sharp blade flashing on its course invokes; I reel with the terror his cool precision and strong swing incites.

The traveller takes the yew wood and uses his knife to strip and carve it – bleeding as yew does – by the fire-light. He sits with his back to the trunk of the tree, one knee up, one leg stretched out and whittles to while away the evening. His face is still, calm, and in his tranquil mood I see the handsome line of his nose, the sturdy angle of his jaw, the gentle soul in those hazel eyes. And I creep closer and darkness falls.

When the yellow glow of fire-light is all that he works by and his hands slow down, his eyelids droop, I smile. I brush my hand along his jowls, feel the prickling of his stubble, run my thumb over his soft lips. I breathe into his neck – my cool, dead breath – in a languid outpouring and the corner of his mouth lifts.

A spark alights within me as I place a hand upon his chest and he is warm to my touch, and firm. My hand is solid and I can feel his heart beat against my palm as though once again I am corporeal. Quickly, I sit astride him, gripping his sides with my thighs, pressing my whole self against him, delighting in my physicality. How real I seem! I push myself against him again, with fervour and he gasps in his sleep, arms reaching to encircle me.

I detach, lose it. I am amazed by our mutual astonishment at the potency – the certainty – of our pleasure.

Willing myself into being, with feet on the ground and the air stirring my hooded cloak, I stand at the edge of the clearing, my focus locked on to him with longing, my white hands reaching.

He glances about, mutters, 'Goddess?' and looks into my eyes.

I know he sees me, feel it as a stab in the breast. Holding his gaze I wipe the tip of my tongue across my lips and move backwards into the woods and feel myself fade away to nothing.

The traveller starts after me, blundering into low hanging branches unseen in the dark then stops, stands still in contemplation. With a shake of his head and a sigh he returns to his camp to pick up his carving, lying in the mulch where he dropped it. It is an effigy of the Goddess. He is creative, this man, has carved her well. Her arms rise above her head where her hands entwine; she has large breasts, a full belly and rounded hips – her legs he has not yet hewn.

I reach for where the pendant hung from my neck in life. My son has it now, and it is very similar to what the traveller makes. If he puts the coiling swirl on her belly and carves her legs just so, then my son would make the connection – see it as a sign. The traveller tucks his unfinished carving into his gear and curls up on his bedroll. And I float out into the night.

I feel the tide of the underground river that tugs at me but I resist. I soar up to the sky and scream until the brittle stars splinter. Mother Earth will swallow me up, take me into her womb so that I can be reborn but I cannot go, I am not ready. Not yet.

I move with the wind through the trees and keep trying,

keep learning to take form and control it. I travel through the woodland and out to the other side, to the clearing on the far side of the hill and there I find my young son and wipe his brow where he sleeps. He is a brave boy and for his sake I evade the inevitable for another night.

At dawn, I return to the traveller and sink down beside him. I prise a slit open so I can creep in under his covers and spoon with him, match my breathing with his. I edge my hand over and feel the heat emanate from him. He is hot with sleep. Slowly I begin to wake him with a gentle caress. His phallus stirs into life at my touch, growing hard as, in an echo, I too take solid shape and form. I laugh deep in my throat as my own arousal begins to pulsate. I am alive!

The traveller opens his eyes – so silent is his awakening that I know only by the way he holds his breath. I withdraw, fingers lingering and he turns with my departure, a pleading fury flashing in his eyes.

I feel my cloak rippling, the damp ground like wet ice beneath my bare feet. I beckon, the movement shifts the folds of fabric, reveals for just a second that beneath it I am naked. He's a grown man, he knows.

In his haste to follow me, the traveller knocks over the stones he gathered to build his fire in.

'Wait!'

I pause and smile then slip away between the shadowy trees, and he growls.

Later, as he is breaking camp, with his gear packed

and his boots scuffing the grey ashes, I wait a few paces off the footpath. He stops and stares.

'Are you the Goddess?' he asks, his quiet voice faltering.

I shake my head, '*No.*'

I turn with a swirl of my cloak, moving so that he can glimpse the pale flesh curving, and want it. I glance back to see him fumbling for his gear, shoving those last possessions in his bag. I go on.

I know that he is following me; I can hear him moving closer. I let my hood fall back and my long hair hangs loose.

'Are you Fey?'

With a toss of my auburn locks, I face him. '*No.*'

I put my fingers to my lips, slowly blow him a kiss. The motion exposes one of my breasts; the edge of the cloak brushing its nipple, crumpling it up. The traveller asks no more questions, only follows.

On I go; sometimes I am near him, other times I am far. Once I sweep past him and as he reaches to catch me his fingers touch mine. But then I am just the wind and the leaves dripping down.

We play this game and I lead him on. I lead him uphill and deeper into the woods and he no longer cares. He follows me over the hill and through the woods until we come out the other side, as the trees thin to let the breeze sweep down the gentle slope before tumbling over the cliffs to the beach where the sea sighs forever. We can just about smell it now, and hear it – the sea and shore's slow embracing.

The traveller stands with his back to me, and I behind him and to the left, watching him gather his bearings. He gazes out at the hillside dropping away to cliff face and beyond he glimpses the smudge of the sea folding into the sky.

Gently, I let my cloak fall to the ground, the softest of sounds. He turns at the rush of fabric cascading and finally he sees what I have been leading him to. It is not I, for I have relinquished my substance.

What the traveller sees is our little horror: the burnt-out cluster of houses that was our settlement. Our homes are misshapen forms of blackened stone and charred frames torn apart, their hearthstones lie in scattered disarray. Ruins they are. The scorched remains of our sheep and our dogs – and some of us – are indistinguishable mounds among the debris. Only patches of the wooden fence remain. Jagged scraps, that once linked to gird our village, hang askew from their great oak posts. They too are burnt to black and smouldered for days after the attack. Now, coal-black crows perch on them and watch. Our village was razed to the ground by marauders who came rolling in with the sea in foreign vessels.

The traveller forgets me as he stares at the silent ruins that in their despair snuff out his lust. He does not even reach for my cloak. The quiet moment quivers with gloom, and the traveller is suspended in shock.

My son bolts from his hiding place, tears from the edge of the woods, thin arms flailing, skinny legs pounding, his shrieks bursting the stasis in a flood of sound and motion. The traveller jolts, crows scramble skyward in a flurry of wing. My boy throws sticks, the traveller backs off.

My son, Elgin, topples forward with the effort of throwing the last of his sticks but it falls short of the traveller. He grabs clumps of new grass that he rips from the earth and tosses at him. The traveller gives him yet more space.

Elgin keeps his blue eyes on him, and edges towards my cloak. He snatches it up with dirty hands, full of cuts and bruises.

My little boy, he alone survived the attack. How hard we ran, how fast we dodged and wove between the trees from those long-legged men with their full beards and their axes glinting. We thought we stood a chance because we ken these woods so well. But there were too many of them, and they were mean. They caught us unawares and cut us down as we fled; every one of us but Elgin. What they wanted from us I cannot fathom, for we were never prosperous.

But when those men had left the settlement ablaze, little Elgin alone crept out and peered from one dead face to the next until he came to mine. He thought to bury us all, but he is just nine years old. My grave was the only one he dug and it is not really deep enough. He piled sticks and rocks and leaves over it and draped my pewter goddess, the one that hung around my neck, on a rowan branch protruding from the top of the mound, and it dangles there.

I could not cross over with the others and embrace death then. I could not leave my child, scratching for food and shelter among the lonely ruins. I could not. I waited, thinking he would not last the week. But he astounds me. He's a bright boy and strong. He copes. He goes on and on my Elgin does.

He sleeps in the hollow of a dying oak tree and he has survived one moon after the next on his own. But autumn is here with winter at her heels and I cannot get him to abandon this place. He will not leave my grave. And I, in turn, will not watch him suffer cold and hunger unto a slow and sorry death. I cannot. I want my son to live and thrive.

I thank the Goddess for sending us the traveller – he is so kind, so gentle. He lingers by the ruins all day. He comes across my grave and stares at the pendant that marks it. Then he gathers wood to build a fire and sets up camp. He delays his own homecoming for the sake of a child who threw sticks at him.

Elgin watches him from the trees as he cooks a meal from his provisions. He's clever, the traveller is, wise and patient. He sits and whittles away at his yew wood and waits for the fragrant promise of pottage to draw my Elgin to him.

And when Elgin at last sits beside him, he sees the effigy of the Goddess and he sees the traveller has carved it to look just like mine, and they begin to talk. They spend a long time discussing many things.

'What did your mother look like?' the traveller asks casually.

Elgin replies, 'My mother was the most beautiful woman in the world.' Then with a little more prodding, he adds, 'Her eyes are like mine and her hair is reddish-brown.'

The traveller smiles and nods, 'Hair like autumn oak leaves, falling.'

He hands the yew goddess to Elgin and lets him hold it, lets him sleep with it.

In the morning they go to my grave and the traveller shows Elgin to place his yew goddess on the top, and taking my pendant, hangs it around Elgin's neck. Elgin clasps it tight and presses it to his lips.

The traveller offers Elgin his hand, and when he takes it my relief is so intense that it rises up in a great wave, lifting me up above the canopy. It sends the leaves — drops of copper and gold — streaming out across the hillside while I drift, suspended high above. Waiting for that tidal pull to find me and haul me slowly in, I watch the traveller and my boy getting smaller and smaller as they walk away together. Going far away to join the clan of the *cors*, to belong there.

A Rose for Paul

Polly Samson

I watched the widow as they lowered Vincent into the earth. Doesn't everyone do that at a funeral? We watch, the widow weeps, and if we're honest we find ourselves longing for something a little more dramatic like suttee. She might wail, or beat her chest, or faint and fall into the grave. No one likes a merry widow. I once saw a woman kiss her second husband beside the grave of her first: it was just a brush of the lips, but I knew. Just as I knew I wasn't the only soul ready to condemn Analise Edmonds for the merest flicker of a smile that morning.

We shivered around the grave pulling collars to the wind. It was perfect: bare and dark, bare trees, bare earth, a sky the colour of wet newspaper and Analise, to her credit, properly pale and thinner than ever; eyes streaming behind the modest veil of an upright black hat. Analise in a long black coat that I might once have bothered to envy, and supported by her boy who was ushering her towards the Astroturf that framed Vincent's final resting place; a nervous horse coaxed by its groom.

From where I was standing I could only see the back of the boy. His stance. Rory was his name: solid as oak, an arm around his mother who had her face pressed to his shoulder. I heard her gasp just once, as the coffin straps delivered Vincent to his underworld with a little whisper of webbing on wood. The priest intoned and a few cold wet drops plopped from the branches above my head and trickled inside my collar. I watched Rory bow his head with its black beanie and red hair fringing over the collar of his coat.

He turned from his mother as a slender girl stepped forward craning her neck to the hole. This girl was swathed in folds of black lace and fishnet, anyone would think she'd come dressed for the opera. I watched Rory hold himself erect, a barrel full of grief in his chest while she clung to him, her hat of black feathers fluttering and curling in the trouble-making breeze.

Other people approached the grave, sprinkling mud, their lips moving in silent incantation; three old ladies – Vincent's aunts, I realised, but grown terribly old, polythene rain hats tied beneath their chins; I lip-read a man in a mac, probably a colleague of Vincent's: 'Goodbye you old bastard,' I swear that's what he said.

There was a rose bush in a black bucket beside the

grave, and I found myself watching Analise and thinking how strange it would be to snip a rose that had been nourished by your loved one's old bones. A couple of years ago a friend of mine had her father incinerated, and when she went to scatter his ashes found herself suddenly unable to resist dabbing just a little bit of it on her tongue to see how it tasted. Ashes to ashes. A sob escaped from the barrel of Rory's chest. Ashes to ashes, bonemeal for roses and thorns from my heart. He brought his sleeve to cover his eyes and Analise reached her hands to him. A rose for a dandy's buttonhole or a stem cut off in its prime, to stand alone on a bedside table. Umbrellas started to go up. I watched frail Analise flanked by Rory and the floozy in the feathered hat whose inexperience of funerals now showed in the sinking heels of her footwear. Glued to Analise's side she was, stroking and patting with a black, lace-gloved hand; no gooseberry would she be. I stifled a smirk as Analise leant away from her feathery tormentor, every cell in her body keening towards her son.

Something made Analise whimper and turn her face into Rory's coat and then my own eyes started to swim as I thought about how much Vincent loved his dog, hairy mutt that it was, and a particular green sweatshirt that he used to wear. Vincent in the sunshine by a river, the day he found the hairy mutt, the way he untangled it from the bushes and briars – shivering, it was only a pup – and held it wrapped in his sweatshirt with a look on his face so tender that remembering it made me cry out. People I barely recognised stared at me. And then realising who I was stared again. I might have been an apparition come back to haunt them.

Analise turned to me. There was nothing I could do but kiss her, I felt the powder from her cheek on my lips and had to surreptitiously wipe them with a tissue. The perfume she wore, the same one, something like hyacinths but yeastier. Then the girlfriend: 'Amelia,' introducing herself. 'Rory's fiancée.' I was glad to see this Amelia was not the sort of girl my boy Paul would have gone for; all panda-eyes she was from the wrong mascara, though she'd learn, all too soon, to wear water-proof to funerals. There was altogether too much bother about her: feathers drooping from the rain, an ivory cameo on a black velvet choker at her throat, even a little hairnet. 'And you are?' She asked, head cocked to one side and one eye on Rory walking away with his arm around his mother. She didn't wait for my answer but managed: 'Vincent will like being right next to the football ground,' before bolting in pursuit of her beau and Analise. My favourite of Vincent's polythene-hatted aunts squeezed my hand: 'No he won't,' she whispered and told me where to go for the wake.

I waited there in the rain for the men to get their shov-els and watched them for a while. Vincent's rosebush was wintering, nothing more than twigs, it would look like the hand of famine reaching from his grave.

A Rose for Paul

I wasn't planning on going to the wake. I took the long way out of the churchyard and, wouldn't you know it, my path took me winding along the avenue where the children's graves are, the cherished angels departed too soon, God's little raindrops, plump moss over a baby's grave like a coverlet of green velvet.

The wake was in a room above a pub. There was the usual veiled nastiness about the will, smoked salmon on squares of buttered brown bread with disdainfully curling edges. I grabbed at toothpick kebabs of cheese and silver-skin onions but was unable to stop myself from seeing those pearly onions as Vincent's eyes in his fatal last bath so had to put them down again. I came face to face with a woman I used to know and commended her reading from *The Wasteland*, though I'd have happily thrown a handful of dust down her throat to stop the garbled torture. I kept an eye on Analise sweeping like a wraith between people. I heard her say: 'Vincent was a good man, you know ... ' And someone else butting in with a memory: 'Vincent drank them all under the table.' 'And another thing ... ' And an old man with a bit of a tremor claiming to be the only surviving male in the family: 'It's the heart gets us all you know.'

I thought about my Paul, the heart in his chest as sweet and pure as a lily. It had been good for my spirits seeing him in Kensal Rise.

I'd gone straight to Kensal Rise from the sleeper. Three hours to kill before the funeral and hardly daring to hope as I rattled around the flat making a cup of tea, talking out loud so that if he was there he'd know it was me. I peered around the corner into the alcove and the sight of him made me catch my breath. Quietly at the table, with his chin resting in his hands, deep in thought. My Paul. He smiled his long, lazy smile as he reached to touch my face with gentle fingers and my heart swelled to see his eyes glinting like opals. It was always the first thing I noticed about Paul: the brightness of his blind eyes. I cradled his dear head and stroked his still baby-soft hair.

My first memory of Paul: a bubble, a hot August night with a full moon burning through our thin curtains. I woke after midnight, a tickling trail all the way up to my chest, like a trickle of sweat but stickier. It was hot in our bedroom, and stuffy: we couldn't open the window because we didn't have the bars fitted and an intruder might have just stepped in. Vincent: 'I'll get the windows done while you're at the hospital. It'll take my mind off it.' Well, I was home from doing his bidding and he hadn't even stayed home, let alone fitted the security bars. The night was stifling. All Vincent said when I heaved myself back through the door was: 'There's blood on your skirt.' Eventually we'd got ourselves to sleep. Vincent didn't dare reach for my hand and I didn't know if I wanted him to anyway; I wished for the world to stop spinning. That's how I thought it would be for ever until I woke with that trickling sensation, thinking maybe I was dreaming. But then I looked down and saw a pulse, as he burrowed his raw little body, this tiny marsupial, smaller than a thumb, snuggling himself right into the folds of me, and instinct took over as I closed myself around him.

'She was married to my father for twenty years!' Rory's voice broke into my thoughts. He was discussing me with the girlfriend and jerking his thumb in my direction. Whatever her name was giggled as Rory twisted round to face me. There was practically a flounce to his coat-tails as he strode forward, and the hairs on the back of my neck stood to attention. The belligerent lips were an exact copy. The bouncing Caravaggio curls. It could have been Vincent himself with that peacock stance, gawping so rudely into my face. Flaming Rory. I'd been expecting it: it might have been a thrill if only it didn't make me feel so sad. He came right up to me, sort of swaggering, and practically bumped me into a corner behind a potted fern. My heart began to thump. Six months younger than my Paul. I could hear the beat of it in my ears. It was enough to make me distrust flame-haired Rory before he even opened his overripe mouth.

'So you're my father's *other* wife.' Too close, his breath stinking of grief and drinking.

'Well,' I say. Not technically true. 'I divorced him before he married your mother.'

'Yeah,' he says and there's a curl to his lip that I know all too well. '*Eventually* you did.' He holds out his hand for me to shake, but when I reach for it puts his thumb to his nose and waggles his fingers. The likeness to Vincent is astonishing. Any minute now this puerile youth, with his reddened wattles and over-polished shoes, might start bragging about the novel he'd not yet written.

That was the thing: there'd been a *magnum opus* lodged inside Vincent the whole time; it had been troubling that he couldn't get it out. Our flat at Kensal Rise was kept quiet as a temple to the god of its gestation. The purity of Vincent's thought was not to be interrupted by the ticks and tocks of conventional clocks. No pram in the hall was supposed to run its wheels back and forth over the fragile embryo of Vincent's *magnum opus*, oh no. And yet here it was, in the flesh: hotheaded Rory, so alive he almost vibrated. 'Sarah, Sarah, Sarah,' he said grabbing me by the arm, then turning to dismiss the girlfriend. 'No one ever spoke your name in our house.'

'Sarah, Sarah, Sarah ... raise your hand if you can hear me.' There'd been trouble with my blood pressure in the hospital recovery room. I could hear what I thought was the hiss of a Bunsen burner, the smell of gas. I floated in and out of consciousness. I was back in the school science lab, looking down the broad, brown stripe of the bench as Mr Godwin came into dreamy focus handing me an egg. Mr Godwin, the Josef Mengele of biology teachers, had declared me the winner of that day's luckless lucky dip. I took the egg. For twenty-one days this Godwin had reached his mortician's fingers into an incubator, making us all sick with dread at its electric ticking. We'd all had to write our names on an egg before he started the incubation. *Tick tick tick* behind our backs in the classroom. He was pushing his glasses up his greasy nose to repeat the name on the egg and beckoning. 'Sarah ...' I cringed my way to where he stood holding the egg between thumb and finger and demanding that I peel it to reveal to the rest of the class the embryo inside.

We'd already seen things we wished we hadn't: hearts beating in jelly, cold cuts in aspic, things that, when cut, instead of blood had runny egg yolk dribbling out. I wasn't as unlucky as some, though we were all made to witness the later travesties in the name of O-level biology. I prodded and snipped with the instruments inside the gory sac with its bloodshot membranes and detached a thing twitching like a large, peeled prawn, and just for a moment I thought I saw its tiny blue heart beating within its transparent chest. I carried it bobbing in a jar into school dinner after the lesson and set it beside me on the table. It floated in its sea of formaldehyde. 'Ugh,' the others said, putting down their forks. 'Why do you have to do that?'

My chickadee only had aniseed-sized specks where his eyes should have been. I shook the jar and the pink thing bounced up and down making my friends squeal. That's what I was thinking about when I finally came round in the hospital.

'So, Sarah, I've wondered about you all my life.' Rory's talking at me as I try to free myself, but he clutches my arm tighter and swipes a glass of white wine from a tray, tipping it to me in mock salutation then taking a gulp. He has the nerve to look me up and down. 'All the photographs of you were burned,' he says.

'Charming,' I say, as I try to pull away. Rory moves his grip to my shoulder, pulling me forward. For one unnerving moment I think he's going to try to kiss me but then he pulls me closer, so close I can smell the wool of his coat and he hisses in my ear: 'You know you shouldn't be here. I don't think you were invited.'

'Rory, stop it,' Analise appears, grabbing the glass from his hand. 'Come and sit down.' She doesn't speak to me at all. I am in little doubt that the kiss at the cemetery was nothing but an aberration but am pleased to confirm from up close that she has the face she deserves with jowls of discontent and pockets of bad temper. 'Come away, Rory.' And a voice that still has the power to chill me to the marrow.

'I've told you already. He's in a meeting.' Cold and clinical as I begged her from the hospital phone to fetch

Vincent. And now she says, as though trying to convince herself: 'He was a good father to Rory,' and the ice cracks beneath the surface: 'Oh Sarah, if only you hadn't told those lies.' And she starts to cry.

Lies! Flames start curling at the base of my throat. Lies? Had I lied about the damage that was done to my Paul to make way for the drunken creature who still has my arm in his grip? 'You've got the family chin,' I tell him and laugh in his face.

I try to push past them but Rory blocks my way. He ignores Analise pleading for him to come with her; he ignores his girlfriend's flapping hands. 'My mother doesn't need to see you. Why don't you go now?' He looks slyly back to Analise. 'Not that I mean to be rude or anything ... ' He lets me go. His lips hang in just the way that I knew they would.

At the hospital I'd been placed in a ward full of women who were having trouble holding on to their babies. They were all clasping their tummies as though that might help keep them in and asking me about mine. 'How many weeks, dear?' they said, gesturing at my still almost-flat stomach. I called home with trembling fingers but there was no reply though Vincent had promised not to go out while this thing was done. In a meeting, Analise coolly informed me when I called the office. No, he could not be disturbed, she said, and I was raw, flayed grief, turning myself inside out.

As I walked from the wake through the rain I tried to

shake the thought of revolting Rory from my head. He
was no more than a peacock rattling its feathers at me.
How horrible the men in that family were. Vincent had
been with a woman who was not Analise on the night
that he died. No one was talking about that.

By the time I got back to Kensal Rise I was soaked
through, rinsed by the rain of almost all my indignation.
I put the key in the lock of our old flat but by then I was
already thinking about the moors and my dogs waiting
for me on the sofas at home. The thump of their tails on
the cushions whenever I passed, the idiocy of their ador-
ing eyes: it was like being a film star in my own
sitting-room as I paced up and down with my notebook
and pencil doing the thing I love to do more than anything else in the world.

I hung my keys on the hook beside Vincent's, still
there like an ornament: a souvenir with a rabbit's-foot
fob. He left one morning while I watched a squirrel
stealing nuts from the bird table. I had my Paul close,
snug between my breasts as any joey in his mother's
pocket. 'It's twenty weeks today,' I called out to Vincent
who was pulling on his socks. 'Our baby is viable.' 'Oh
for God's sake, you're never going to stop this nonsense,'
he said, as he flung down his keys and slammed the
door.

I wondered, because I couldn't help it, whether any of
my books had ever found their way across Vincent's
desk at the *Daily Mail* where he wrote mainly about

boob jobs and cellulite, *his magnum opus* as dead to him as his soul. I stepped into the kitchen shaking rain from my hair and Paul came shimmering towards me, pale and beautiful. He lifted his hands to my face. As we embraced, I vowed I would spend more time in town come the summer: I would visit Vincent's grave and cut a rose for Paul. It was quite a cheery thought. I had a perfectly lovely pair of secateurs at home.

On the Turn of the Tide

Jacky Taylor

Out in the curve of the bay, a woman is walking. She takes several short steps, stops, bends down to the sand, sways right and left, then rises up like a finger of dark.

Ellory Temple is listening to the stones. Where sand and pebbles meet is where she finds them. It is not easy to discern which are the ones that will speak to her, she has to look carefully, assess their shape, feel them in her palm, but she knows that if she treats them with respect they will tell her secrets. Curling her fingers round their sea-beaten smoothness, she can feel them thrum – the ones that will talk. She gathers them gently into the folds of her skirt, cradles and lulls them with the rock of her step as she makes her way further along the shore.

She picks up clumps of beaded bladder-wrack to nest them. The larger stones she ignores, it's the smaller ones that hold her interest, but she has to catch them at the right moment. If they have been worn too thin by time, their voices will be too weak for her to hear and their stories will be lost; she cannot help them. This is a sorrow to her and a burden, but there is nothing she can do to prevent it: it is willed.

Sometimes they will warn her of things to come, but that is a rarity. The seeing stones, these are the most precious and difficult to find, often lying hidden by the edges of rock pools or buried under plastic containers and the mounds of detritus ejected from ships in the channels. The oldest are secretive and know how to hide; they've had centuries to practise. Holding all that they've seen, all that they know, they keep it within themselves waiting, waiting ...

And when eventually they have told their stories they will shed their stony husks, let the sea reclaim them and grind them to sand. The voices will drift on as the updraught catches them. They will rise to circle in the thermals and jostle with the cries of gulls. Some will ride on their backs, just for the pleasure of it, until the wind carries them away over sea, forest and mountain, invisible as atoms stretching to oblivion.

Every morning Ellory retreads her steps, moulds her footprints back into the sand, always searching. Some call her mad and warn their children to stay away. 'Funny old girl,' they say, 'best keep your distance, no telling what she might do.' Others say she's harmless, just a lonely woman the years have forgotten to be kind to – 'it's living on your own, it does things to you.' Talk was of her having lost someone, though no one could remember who or when that might have been.

The disapproving continue to tut behind their curtains, the rest leave her be save for the odd one or two. These few utter good mornings with urgency, embrace each day afresh, and each day frown in bewilderment when she scowls in response.

Ellory stays clear of them all and they, for the most part, stay clear of her. But there are the boys, now they're another kettle of fish entirely and one of them's up there on the hill. She picks up one of the stones from her skirt and holds it to her ear. Freezing her face in concentration she nods once, slowly, then turns her gaze up towards the sandy knoll.

Cam is watching her from behind a dune, the sun-bleached tufts of marram twining themselves into his hair. When he's there with his mates, they call out, taunt her with names and obscenities. Sniggering into their sleeves, they kick over the sand looking for pieces of flotsam from the container ships. Joey Blouter's made a slingshot from a frayed piece of marine twine and a curve of broken float. He brings it with him when they gather there and everyone takes turns to score on the moving target; Ellory has the marks to prove it. Cam always misses on purpose, he's tried putting the others off too, though it only turns him into a bull's-eye instead. But today Cam is alone, just watching. He has seen the woman picking at the beach this way before and wants to know what she's doing. All his mates tell him she's bonkers, he half believes it himself, but something else is nagging at the back of his mind and he wants to know what it is.

Kneeling up behind the long grass, he stretches to get a better view of her. He can see her picking things up from the beach, he thinks it might be driftwood – he knows it makes good kindling – but he can't see anything sticking out like it should. What is it she's carrying?

Joey says she just collects any old crap.

'She makes stupid sculpture things and sells them in her garden. All the holiday lot buy them. My dad even bought one for my mum – she nearly hit the roof. Just a pile of junk she said and she's right – I've seen them, they're rubbish.' They all laughed at that.

Cam can see she's being choosy, picking some things to add to her collection, while others are tossed away. Secret things, small enough to hold in your palm and he wants a better look; he wants to know what they are. He had a collection once, he used to keep it in a box under his bed: mermaid's purses, razor shells, crab husks, ammonite fossils, a can with funny writing on and once, a piece of stinking kelp. His mother threw it all out when the reek of seaweed reached the top of the stairs, but Cam misses the salty stench of it.

Creeping out from behind the dune commando style, he edges his way closer.

With a hardly perceptible incline of her head Ellory shows that she's noticed. She knew someone was watching her and felt the shift in the air that company always brings. Squinting her eyes with her head still lowered to the sand, she wonders who the slithering boy is making his way down the slope. Ever so careful he's being and she laughs at him under her breath. These boys, with their dirty words and missiles, why she's half a mind to— But she thinks again, they are just children poking a stick at the adult world they are already fearful of entering. Just boys. No matter then, she'll leave him be. Let him come closer if he wants, he'll be none the wiser after all.

She carries on sorting, watching the boy from the corner of an eye, listens out till she can hear him breathing. He's near now, taking refuge behind the boulder in the rock pool, strands of his fair hair quivering in the wind against the dark granite, and the stone she keeps lifting to her ear is talking.

'Hey, boy. If you really want to see, you'd better come out from behind that rock. You'll get nothing through solid stone now, will you.'

She hears the sharp intake of breath as he gasps, chuckles to herself and waits to see if he's a runner or a lingerer. Thirty seconds and he hasn't flown yet.

'I don't bite you know and I haven't got a slingshot

either. So, are you coming out or not?' Ellory knows boys are like horses, you can hold out a carrot but you have to give them space and wait for them to come to you. This one's mane is as bleached as a palomino, a proud and wild creature, he could bolt at the slightest thing; but he's curious, oh yes he's curious all right. She's pretty sure that'll keep him here, at least until he's got some of what he came for. He's not come out yet, but give it time, just a little patience is all.

'Oh well, suit yourself. I've got things to be getting on with, cheerio then.' She turns her back to the rock and begins to walk away, swaying this way and that as she returns to surveying the stones. Only two steps and she feels the boy's tread in the sand, but she won't turn back, not yet. She starts to hum to herself, a little sound barrier that says *don't worry, I'm staying in my space*, and it works.

'What are you doing? What's that you're collecting? My mates all think you're bonkers. Are you bonkers? You look bloody bonkers.'

'And it's very nice to meet you too I'm sure.' Still she doesn't turn. *Wait for him to come to you.* Cam circles her, sidling in a wide arc at first, but as Ellory hums away he edges closer and the distance between them decreases. Soon he is standing in front of her.

'Ah, there you are. Right, now what is it that you're wanting young man, eh?'

Cam can't quite believe he's so close to her. As her

head bobs up and down with her beach-combing, he catches glimpses of her face and it's not what he expected. He thought she'd be granny age, but she looks younger, more like Mum and Dad.

'What are you doing? What are you looking for? Are you making one of your sculpture things again?'

Ellory raises her head to him. 'Sculpture things? Oh, you mean my weather-tellers. No, no, I'm not looking for those, not now anyway.'

'Well what are you looking for then?'

'Oh, just this and that.'

But Cam doesn't believe her, he knows she's seeking something out, a very particular something and he wants to know what it is.

He follows her and the two of them travel along the foreshore, the strange, swaying woman and the two-steps-behind boy. As the sea moves in to fill the marks they have made in the sand, a scattering of gulls wheel over their heads calling to each other as they eye the waves.

The two begin to climb, easing their way up across the dunes, Ellory letting out little puffs as the going gets steeper. It's harder with the stones, but she knows how to lean her weight and tread on the balls of her feet to stop the sand shifting. When she reaches the top, she keeps to the marram grass, glad to have something firmer under her feet.

'Not far now, nearly home.' She can still hear his

breathing, light and quick as he darts up the incline. After following a narrow path fringed with pebbles and sea kale – forcing its way up between them – they come to a dead end, a tangle of driftwood and rusty wire barring their way.

'Short cut. Mind where you tread, you don't want any of those barbs scraping your skin.' Ellory shifts the wood on to the wire, climbs over, bundling her skirt away from it, and stops to see if the boy will follow. Cam hesitates on the other side.

'This is my garden, you can sit in it if you like while I take these inside. It's up to you, but if you do come, make sure you put the driftwood back as it was. I don't like strangers getting too close.'

She carries on towards the cottage, pausing every now and then to pick a leaf from a plant, pop a berry into her mouth and hold her hand to her ear as if she is listening to something.

Cam waits until she is out of sight then skims the barrier as if he had springs on his feet. He turns round again and moves back a step to replace the wood just as she'd asked him to.

This new place looks strange, but feels safe and he likes the garden. There are things growing everywhere. He doesn't know what half of them are, but he loves the colours and the higgledy-piggledy way they tumble over each other. To the left, past rows of strawberry plants, he can see the sculptures Joey Blouter made them laugh about. Weather-tellers, the woman called them. He walks towards them, runs his palm along the grain of their wood, feels how the sea has weathered it so it feels like his mum's silk blouse. His fingers trail back and forth enjoying the sheer pleasure of touching it. At the tip of each one of these strange creations is a wheel of hanging shells and he spins them all in turn, setting off a gentle clattering and the flip-flap of wooden wings from the carved birds perched on their tops. He recognises each one from its detail: kittiwake, herring gull, cormorant, fulmar and albatross. He thinks Joey Blouter's an idiot, he thinks these things are beautiful. When a sudden gust of wind crosses the garden, a low hum blows through them like a murmur.

Cam moves further into the garden, walks among tall stems of rosebay willowherb that have elbowed their way in between clusters of Echinops and sea-holly. Their downy tufts brush against his hair dislodging seeds that cling to his fringe. Everywhere he looks something is growing. He recognises marigolds with their egg yolk yellows and the regal purples of the lavender bushes, but so much is new to him. He wishes his garden was like this instead of all gravel chippings and wood bark; nothing grows there except for the dandelions heaving themselves up between the fence and next door.

This place is a wonder to him and he breathes it all in, stopping every pace or so to sniff at the flowerheads as he makes for the cottage door, trailing his arms out behind him like wings.

'Well come on in, I won't bite.' Cam hovers over the threshold, holding back until his eyes have lost those blinking dots of light. Ellory is standing by a table, busying herself unloading things from her skirt.

'Come in, come in.' She beckons to him, then waves an arm over towards a bowl sitting on a chair seat. 'Have a strawberry. They're good, you know.' Cam dips his fingers into the bowl and pulls out a fat, bright fruit. He takes a bite, slithers the seed side on to his tongue and sucks the juice back to his throat. His taste buds prick up as he mashes the pulp with his teeth and swallows.

'Go on, have another. I've plenty more.'

Cam helps himself to the fattest one in the bowl and as Ellory laughs at his choice, the corners of his mouth start to turn up.

The woman carries on sorting through the morning's finds; he can't quite see what they are, but the *chink-chink* sound of them knocking against each other and the thud as they are placed on the table tells him they're just stones. Pebbles from the beach is all she's been collecting, just pebbles.

He begins to wander round the room, scanning every which way. There are shelves against one of the walls, full of books and odd things gathered in clusters: birds' skulls, shells, bright glass beads, a child's photograph. Dried plant stems hang down from the ceiling, their seed heads rattling as the woman moves beneath them. There's something interesting in every part of the place and it excites his interest to look at it all. It's as topsy-turvy as the garden, but not messy exactly, not like his bedroom at home that his mum's always complaining about. No, it feels right for it to be this way – he can't explain it, but he's sure everything is where it ought to be; everything, except for something dark lying over the back of an armchair.

As Cam moves towards it, the hairs on the back of his arms start to prickle with static and Ellory hears the stones calling.

'What's this?' Cam's curious, but he doesn't want to get too close.

Ellory stares at the table. This has never happened before. It's supposed to be one stone at a time, but all of them are talking at once, their words jumbling around with such force they are making her head spin.

'Just a minute, young man.' She goes over to the table and like a mother chiding her unruly children, calls for quiet. 'One at a time now, one at a time.' She listens to each one in turn, nods and stares at Cam, then goes out of the room.

He takes a look at the stones for himself. He can't see anything special about them; they're not unusual colours and none of them even have interesting shapes. They wouldn't have made it into his collection that's for sure.

There's a scraping sound coming from the kitchen and a fatty smell he recognises but can't place. The woman is melting something in a pan and stirring it round with a metal spoon.

'Metal's a conductor, you'll burn yourself on that, you will.'

'Well I'll be careful then, won't I.' Ellory smiles at his warning.

'You should be using a wooden spoon, even I know that.' He thinks this woman must be bonkers after all.

'Ah, but not for this. The wood would soak too much of it up and I need every drop.'

'What for?'

'You'll see.'

'What is it anyway? It smells like butter.'

'That's because that's what it is. Now, mind out, I'm coming through and you don't want to burn yourself now, do you?'

Ellory comes out of the kitchen carrying a small saucepan. She puts it down on a table beside the old armchair and fetches a piece of cloth from a bag underneath. Dipping it first into the melted butter, she begins to draw it over the object hanging over the back of the chair. She rubs the cloth lightly in small circles, going round and round until it begins to stick, then dips the cloth back into the pan and begins again.

'What are you doing? What is that thing?'

'Just one of my chores is all. Have to rub the butter

well in to keep it supple you see or it would dry out, and it's no good to anyone then.'

Cam still hasn't had an answer, he wants to know what that thing is.

'Keep what supple? Tell me what it is.'

Ellory lifts the cloth away from the surface and straightens her back. She takes in a breath and as she lets it out her shoulders seem to fall from the weight of it. She turns to Cam.

'You want to know what this is?' Cam nods. 'All right, but not a word, not a sound to another living soul, cross your heart and spit in your palm. Right?' He nods again, crosses his heart and spits as she says; the gravity of his expression tells her all she needs to know.

'This here is a selkie skin.'

'A what?'

'A selkie skin my boy. A rare and precious thing. It belongs to a creature, a seal who can take human form and walk around like you and me, but without anyone knowing. This is from a young one, rarer still, selkies usually only come ashore when full grown.'

Cam thinks this might be another bit of her bonkers talk, but whatever that thing really is he wants to go over and touch it. He edges closer, screws up his eyes so he can peer at it more closely. The small curved section at the top is a mix of grey and browny shades, like the colours of his football socks. Further down, where the skin widens, the colours become mottled and different shades are all mixed in together as if someone has taken a paintbrush and blobbed the colours on to it.

He can see tiny hairs sticking up in places where the woman has been rubbing with her cloth; some are light at the base and grow dark at the tip, while others start off dark and change to light. There are also patches of chalky browns in between, the colours you can see at the base of the cliffs or in the feathers of this year's new gulls. Where the light shines on it, it has a sheen like wet slate. He remembers using pieces of it for windows in sand-castles when he was smaller; fetching buckets of sea for the moats, drops would splash up and make it glisten just like this.

'Can I touch it?'

Ellory eyes him, looks at him hard. 'Only if you're gentle, mind. Remember it's a rare and precious thing, not belonging to us. Its owner will come back for it one day and if we damage it, it will not go well.'

'I won't do anything, I'll be careful. I just want to stroke it.' He extends his arm, reaching out his fingers to draw them down along the skin and shudders with pleasure as he touches it.

'There now, that's something you've never done before, eh? Nor any of those friends of yours. Now don't breathe a word of it. Just a secret between you and me.'

Cam shakes his head and, as he speaks, trails his fingers over and over. 'But what are you doing with it?'

'It was found, on the beach. Not by me, not first I wasn't, but the one who was passed it on to me so to speak. I've been looking after it ever since. The selkie'll be searching, you know.'

'But how will they know that you've got it? How can they get it back?'

'Oh they'll know, and then they'll come and fetch it so they can return to the sea. It's where they belong, it's their home just like mine is here in this cottage and yours is in the village. Without it they're trapped in the human world and that's not good for a selkie. Everything needs to be in its rightful place, everything needs to balance.'

Ellory continues her work on the skin, Cam watching her rubbing and dipping the cloth until the pan is empty, all the while holding his fingers at the edge of it.

'All done. I'll get rid of this now and make us a cup of tea, then I expect you'd best be getting home. Don't want to worry your mother now.' She goes off into the kitchen, busies herself washing the pan and running water for the kettle. She starts to hum to herself, puts the kettle on the stove and brings down a tin from a shelf. Taking off the lid she fetches out two home-made biscuits. She makes a pot of tea, puts it on a tray along with milk, sugar, cups and the biscuits.

'There now, this should set you on your way—' But when she turns into the room the boy has gone; so too has the selkie skin.

Jacky Taylor

Out in the bay if you listen between the wind's whistling, the sound of a mother calling to her son can be heard before the roar of the waves drowns her summoning.

Pandian Uncle and his Ghosts

Anita Sivakumaran

When Pandian Uncle said Babu was killed by a ghost, nobody believed him at first. They said he was spinning ghost stories out of his bum crack as usual, and laughed at him, both behind his back and in front of his face.

Babu was a boy none of us knew very well, but he became famous after his death, because of the mystery surrounding it. He was found shortly after dawn one day, under the Puyalaru Bridge, his dark head bobbing, the bridge girders cutting rectangular shadows on his floating body. Many years ago Puyalaru river used to be full of water, but now it only had little puddles, and the water never washed away even the bits of bones and ash from the burnt corpses. How did Babu come to be floating face down in a mere puddle of water a two-year-old could have waded across without slipping? He had been

in the pink of health. His own mother affirmed he had
not suffered from any ailment of a sort that might have
given him dizzy spells. He had enjoyed a hearty dinner
the previous night and had grabbed a couple of mangoes
for a pre-dawn breakfast. There was no logical explana-
tion for what had happened, so one tended towards a
supernatural one, even if it was from Pandian Uncle,
who was known to have been peculiar since the day he
was born.

Pandian Uncle was my grandmother's third child.
They say the more a mother struggles during labour –
the more painful it is and the longer it takes – the more
she will love her child. Pandian Uncle slid out like a
fish, without a murmur from Granny. He was extremely
pale and sickly, and contracted a severe scalp disease a
month after his birth. The soft downy birth hair fell off
in clumps and sores erupted all over his head. No one
had seen such sores in one so young. Soon he contracted
diarrhoea and a worm infestation and became anaemic.
Granny was aghast. She had to look after her other two
children, the house and the fields. To top that, her husband, Mr Intelligent, got her pregnant immediately after
Pandian Uncle was born and then left on an extensive
motorcycling tour to Meghalaya with seven friends.

Granny told Great Granny that she'd had enough with
the sickly new baby, and wished it dead. These things
sometimes happened, even though it was unthinkable to
consider a child anything but a god's incarnation, and

the idea of a mother not caring about her child was as foreign as America. Some women got tired of bearing children and started hating them, especially when they were sickly. No one acknowledged it; the movies didn't show it.

Great Granny told Granny that she would take charge of this particular child, and to get on with her other work and forget about him.

Armed with milk from her best cow, gingili oil, extracts from box-thorn, sessile, joy-weed, neem, tulsi, curry leaves and unnamed herbs from overgrown fallow lands surrounding the village, Great Granny set to work on her great-grandson. Within a year, colour came to his cheeks and pale wispy hair started growing on his head. Though still bony, he started walking and talking and holding his food down. Bowel movements became regular, the stools solid, his cries stronger and more demanding. Great Granny took care of him like a rare ornamental plant, whose nourishment she developed into an exact science.

As a result, Pandian Uncle turned into a moderately healthy young man, with characteristic pale complexion, cat eyes and a sensitive digestive system. He was extremely conscious, growing up, that one could fall sick any time, and did his best to prevent that occurrence. If someone caught a cold, he refused to even look at that person, much less talk to them, till it went away. He never attended funerals, and stayed next to the giant rotating fans (that would disperse the germs) during weddings. He kept a special pillow, a special straw mat and a special blanket that he stored in the daytime on a separate shelf. No one was allowed to use them. If an overnight guest, by mistake, slept on his mat, he rinsed it with boiling water and hung it on the terrace to dry, keeping close watch in case a monkey or a crow alighted on it. He soaked his blanket and pillow cover in Dettol for a few hours if anyone else used them.

Pandian Uncle had another obsession apart from his health. Ghosts. He sincerely believed that all the ghosts in the ghost world had a peculiar penchant for him. And that they constantly came up with cunning little traps to catch him, which he avoided by using his ingenious brain and also through sheer good fortune. He knew that, contrary to popular belief, ghosts were not sluggish and inactive during daytime, so he kept both his eyes open for anything suspicious that might be a clever trap laid by a nasty ghost.

He never dressed completely in white, for that was the colour of clothing favoured by ghosts. The midday sun might throw a haze over his mind to make him believe he was a ghost himself if he wore white. He never looked down into wells to ascertain the depth of the water, as a well ghost might fix his eyes and draw him in, making him forget how to swim. Instead, he threw a stone in and counted rapidly till he heard a *plonk*, and ascertained the depth by the number he had reached. He never lunched under a tree, as tree spirits were especially mischievous at high noon. In fact, high noon was a dangerous time to be out at all, so he made sure he was always indoors from twelve to three in the afternoon, just to be on the safe side.

At night, his precautions took on a militaristic tone. He made sure that in the event that a spirit possessed the person sleeping next to him, it didn't have easy access to his body. Spirits, like lice, could jump from hair to hair. So while everyone else slept in a row, all heads toward east or west, he lay with his head toward the south. Under no circumstances would he sleep with his head facing north, for that was all evil spirits' direction of origin. He always slept with his foot-wear near his head and a broom at his feet; they were first-rung defence against a ghost looking for a host. Another defence was his dog Johnny, whose ears were antennae that could tune into ghost frequency. It barked when it tuned into a ghost, and it barked frequently.

'If you meet a stranger who looks suspicious,' he told Karthik, Anand, Pappi, me and any other village children who were around, 'always check his feet. If they are turned inside out, it's definitely a ghost.'

He only allowed us to pet Johnny if we listened to his lectures without giggling. He told us why ghosts existed and enumerated the different kinds that one might encounter in everyday life.

'When a person dies malcontent, that is to say, if they

have some unfulfilled wish at the time of their death, they are unable to enter the state of *Moksham*, or be reborn, and are destined to wander the gap between life and rebirth as ghosts till their wish is fulfilled. Here they roam, crazy with grief, hating and envying us humans because they can't be like us. Some of them are mischievous, and some are downright evil. In the main, they try to scare us and make our lives miserable.

'Male ghosts normally wander about, disturbing no one, alone and in utter despair. They do not have the least interest in making themselves manifest to us. Most are content to hang upside down from trees (the favoured ones being tamarind and drumstick). Ghosts of little children abound, but they can be easily fooled. Although, since they are children, they can be unseemly cruel. The most sociable ones, the ones really after you, are the female ghosts. They are, for some reason or other, extremely malcontent. And prefer male victims.

'How to identify the female ghost? It will always wear a completely white sari, and its hair will be untied. The feet will, of course, be inside out. It will have a peculiar ringing laugh, with which it would signal its arrival. But beware. These days, one shouldn't be too surprised when one encounters a female ghost in coloured clothing. Even in silksari-chudithar-salwaarkameez. It's best to be prepared for any eventuality.'

There was a ghost Pandian Uncle was particularly terrified of. The Puyalaru Bridge ghost. It was the most vicious kind of ghost there is, one that liked to suck out all the blood of its victim. A vampire ghost. And this particular vampire ghost especially lusted after a very eligible virgin male's blood: Pandian Uncle's.

He narrated a spine-tingling tale of how the Puyalaru Bridge ghost, aka Bridju Katteri, almost caught him.

When he was sixteen years old, he had been a lean-muscled, fast-moving, hot-blooded teenager, the apple of all the village's young girls' (and ghosts') eyes. His pale eyes and white skin and aquiline nose making him look like a foreigner, hence extra desirable.

Everyone at home except for Great Granny and him had gone to Thiruvannamalai lamp festival to witness the lighting of the Holy Lamp. Great Granny had said she would stay and guard the house. Five hundred seed coconuts were stored downstairs and forty-five marakkas of seed rice lay tied up in gunny sacks on the terrace, and someone needed to keep an eye on them.

Pandian Uncle opted to keep Great Granny company. He knew there would be at least a million people thronging the streets of Thiruvannamalai, vying for a glimpse of the Holy Lamp. Even if he didn't catch some sort of contagious disease, he was sure to be crushed to death by some fat, overpious housewife.

That day, Singaram and Alli from the neighbouring Vadacheri village had invited both of them for a special evening worship at their Sivan temple, followed by a street-show. Great Granny, an hour before they were about to leave, experienced a bout of dizziness, and decided to stay at home. So Pandian Uncle went on his own, only the Raleigh bicycle for company.

Of course it was common knowledge that you had to cross the Puyalaru Bridge to go into Vadacheri, but at four in the afternoon, the Bridju Katteri didn't seem to be particularly dangerous, and Pandian Uncle calculated he would return by eight o'clock.

When he reached Vadacheri, he found that it was a much bigger celebration than he had imagined. He also discovered the reason behind the special worship and the entertainment. The new Village Board colour TV. The puja was an elaborate affair. Five priests sat around a fire pouring ghee. The TV was blessed, along with the cattle, harvest, elders and the commons. The entertainment was a puppet show, in which two comedians spoke bad language, plunging the village children into hysterics. It was a classic Big Strong Man kicking the stuffing out of Small Silly Man, and sometimes Silly Man getting cheap thrills out of conning Strong Man.

After the puppet show, which taught Pandian Uncle more synonyms for 'bum' and 'cock' than he cared to know, the TV was brought to the big temple yard with great fanfare, a hired video player produced, and the super-duper hit film *Nayakkan* was screened. Every woman, man, child and infant was present to watch the film on the first colour TV set they had ever seen. There were even people from the neighbouring villages, for Vadacheri's was the first Panchayat council to have bought a colour TV in the entire North Arcot district.

The BPL FWR 21 was sleek grey, with a gently curved screen, and buttons instead of the old knobs. The film was superb. Some people watched the entire movie without blinking (another symptom of a ghost infection) and with parted mouths. Even Pandian Uncle dared not blink lest he miss even a single expression on Kamalakasan's face (even the white *veshti* the actor wore in the film dripped emotion). Such was its magic, that when it was over, Pandian Uncle was quite shocked to find it was close to midnight.

Now he would have spent the night in Vadacheri quite gladly, dusted off a corner of the temple yard and folded his shirt into a pillow, but Great Granny was expecting him. If he crossed the bridge to go home, there was a good chance that the Katteri would kill him, but paradoxically, if he didn't go, Great Granny would think the Katteri had killed him and be really worried. Also, he wanted to make sure Great Granny hadn't fallen terribly ill in the course of the evening. One had to keep a constant eye on old people or they dropped off like flies when one wasn't looking.

The gathered people, scandalised at how late it was, disappeared into their homes. Only Pandian Uncle and his trusty Raleigh were left, and the bicycle gave him a little hope.

If he cycled really fast, he thought, he would be up and across the bridge without the Katteri even noticing.

So then, night-time. Not a single soul stirred. Animals are, of course, soulless. But it was only the Brothers in the convent school in which he studied who said that. Didn't the Hindu scriptures say animals had souls? Or was it James Herriot? The vet's story was the only one he had read in his *Tenth Standard English Non-detailed Reader* before he ran away from the convent. Surely dogs had souls. They were more loyal than humans could ever be. He thought his dog Johnny would give its life to save his. But then, Johnny was quite a distance away, outside their house at the very end of Marapattu. But, happily, Marapattu jurisdiction began right at the spot where the bridge ended. Oh how he wished he were already across that bridge. He would buy Johnny fifty *paise*'s worth of butter biscuits if he made it across safely.

The road was lined with sugar-cane fields. The wind whooshed through the leaning canes. He shut his ears to the sound. But now the bridge loomed white and tremendously long in the chill moonlight, and the only dogs about were pariah dogs that howled to the moon. Didn't they say dogs howled when they sensed evil spirits? Uncle's courage ebbed as he neared the bridge. Sweat trickled underneath his collar, creeping down his back like cold little fingers.

The cycle tyres touched the cement bridge that

seemed to float milkily above the low river. A rank smell of long-burnt corpses wafted over, filling Uncle's throat. The rotating spokes whirred above the concrete, playing percussion to the *swish swish* of the air cutting through the girders. Pandian Uncle pedalled furiously. He was passing the halfway point and was relaxing just a little bit, thinking maybe he had been a bit too hasty in promising a whole fifty *paise* for the dog, when he heard the cackle: the Katteri, delighted to have spotted him.

They say, with good reason, that when you are fleeing from a ghost, you should never turn back to look. The horror of the ghost's appearance will freeze you in one spot so the ghost can stop running (or flying) and simply take its time, saunter towards you, adjust the crease of its sari-falls on the way if it pleases, even smoke a *beedi* if it is a ghost with bad habits, before plucking you from your frozen spot like a feather off a chicken.

Pandian Uncle pedalled like a devil himself, though his pounding heart told him it was so much easier to just stop, catch his breath, have a little rest and cultivate a fatalistic attitude. But he kept his legs pumping, and he was almost at the end of the bridge, had almost made it to safety when an insane feeling of curiosity tapped on his shoulder and made him turn his head. The cycle stopped even though he hadn't applied the brakes.

The Bridju Katteri wore a blood-stained white sari, and floated a few metres above the surface of the bridge. She was ten feet away, and still cackling. Her hair curled all around her, looking like it hadn't been oiled or brushed in months, and she had a fang at either corner of her mouth (very useful for puncturing the skin of an unresisting human neck). Her eyes were enormous and transfixing. She seemed delighted to have found, at last, a virile virgin boy to appease her woman's blood-lust.

The Bridju Katteri hovered closer as Uncle sat half-twisted and fully frozen on his bicycle seat. She made a hissing sound and reached a long curving arm, whose pointy-nailed fingers curled through the air like tendrils of smoke towards Uncle's succulent self.

As the nail of her forefinger skimmed the skin of his neck, reaching for a hold, a sound startled both of them.

It was, miracle of miracles, Johnny, standing with his ears pointing to the moon and feet apart in an attacking stance. He barked his fierce bark, waking Pandian Uncle from his stupor. Uncle withdrew his neck in the nick of time from the Katteri's grasp, and pedalled.

Johnny made a leap forward and growled at the Katteri, who shrank from the fearsome beast. In a flash, even as he thrust his shivering foot on the pedal, Pandian Uncle realised that animals had souls that were stronger than some ghosts' spirits. He pedalled furiously through Marapattu even though he knew the Katteri couldn't come after him, for her powers only extended the length of the bridge. He collapsed with relief when he reached the house and saw Great Granny snoring on her cot.

*

He was always teaching us ways to outsmart ghosts.

'If a ghost tried to step in water,' he said, 'it would start melting.'

'If there is a ghost trying to catch you,' he advised us, 'jump into the nearest water body, even if it's tea in a cup.'

We all tittered and said, 'Stupid Uncle, how can anyone jump in a tea cup?'

He shushed us angrily and said, 'What do you know, you little devils, how serious the matter of the ghosts is?'

He said that if one observed closely, with plenty of concentration, one would realise that the well ghost only hovered above the water, making the impression that it was in the water. Or it simply sat or stood on the last step or on a protruding branch or brick above the water level.

The Bridju Katteri, he said, clung to the underside of the bridge, with one ghostly ear pressed against the concrete. She knew someone was on the bridge by the vibrations they made, and crawled out to attack them, presenting the illusion that she rose from the riverbed.

The night on the bridge, when the Bridju Katteri's nail grazed the skin on the back of Uncle's neck, she got a taste of his blood, and it had intensified her hunger by a thousandfold. When he escaped, by the skin of his teeth, or neck in this case, saved by the dog, her disappointment, in consequence, was thousandfold. Hence the anger that stemmed out of this disappointment was also thousandfold, and that in turn increased her blood-lust for this particular virile virgin by a thousandfold.

'She is after me,' he said with a shudder. 'She cannot rest till she drinks my blood. Her thirst is gouging her throat like acid. And the thirst is not just for my blood, it is also for revenge, for I insulted her by not succumbing to the caress of her fingernail.'

It was tempting to believe that Babu's death was the handiwork of the Bridju Katteri. In the days that followed, Pandian Uncle slowly found an audience willing to believe in his ghost narratives. He said Babu must have seen the ghost and jumped into the water to escape her, and then, who knew what happened? Maybe she got to him by telepathy. Maybe she hopped on stones. Or maybe she transfixed him on the bridge itself, then threw him into the water. He told many a captivated villager how he had narrowly escaped the Katteri during the night of the Vadacheri Village Board's film screening, and how, even in the middle of the day, whenever he had to cross the bridge, he could hear an angry hiss almost on the skin of his neck as he pedalled across at a tearing pace.

Suddenly, people seemed to remember an odd feeling, why yes, a someone-breathing-down-your-neck sensation when they crossed the bridge at night. Velu of Top Street recalled an eerie cackle once when he had to cycle to Vadacheri in the dead of the night.

Kutti Karuppan, who studied in the government

school, let out a secret that he had kept resolutely for many months. He had to cross the bridge every day to go to school. Once his mother had packed him a lunch of roasted goat liver. That day, when he opened his box at lunch-time, salivating well in anticipation of the treat, the goat livers, every one of the six, had disappeared. His mother had packed his lunch in front of his eyes, and he had kept the lunch bag on his lap the entire morning for fear that one of his classmates would open his box in a fit of curiosity. But they were missing all the same. The mystery had been inexplicable until now. It could only have been the work of the Bridju Katteri. And it all fitted; it made sense. The Katteri's blood-lust, and the fact that the goat liver was encrusted with blood (though it wasn't very fresh blood; it was congealed, fried and packed with condiments).

So, slowly, for the lack of any other evidence, and also because this made a far more entertaining story, hardy enough for several retellings, the whole village came to believe that Babu's death was the handiwork of the Bridju Katteri. And in a village where dogs were considered pariahs, Johnny became a hero.

Obeah Blue

Jacqueline Crooks

You always believed he was an obeah man – the way he left his body at night, travelling great distances through digital landscapes, ganja smoke swirling, dub *riddims* pounding speaker boxes. Rimshot thunder shaking the walls like a Cockpit Country storm.

It is midnight and you are sitting in his study, in the basement. You relight the yellowing spliff and swallow its sweetness with a grateful 'raaasss.'

His framed photographs of stones and lichens are still hanging on the damp walls; his phosphorescent green eyes staring out from a self-portrait. You have his emails, one a month for the past three months.

You need to know, want to learn from these silent images. Has he drifted off into the grave-dust darkness of his pictures?

Is ho *really* dead?

You click on the laptop and look through the three emails from duppydigital@eastlight.com

You suck harder on the spliff: '*aahhhhhhh.*' Holding the earthy flavour of other worlds in the back of your throat, you close your eyes as you are projected into his photos of swirling smoke and shifting sand patterns. Your body obeah blue with remembering.

He had rented a cottage on the uninhabited Isle of Rona to take pictures for a forthcoming exhibition. He stared out from the doorway of the Mission House cottage that overlooked the tidal bay of Dry Harbour. Earlier you had walked together in the frosty afternoon light, taking photographs of sand ripples, moss and lichen.

'Don't let the spirits skank you, baby,' he said. A council estate white-bwoy-rude-bwoy made good, he spoke the language of urban, hard-core realities. 'When the darkness comes,' he said, 'I'm gonna dissect it with my camera.' He turned and came towards you, smiling as he led you into the bedroom.

In bed, he lit a spliff. You opened your mouth for a blow-back of hallucinatory hashish.

He caressed your breasts as he shaped his white body around your brown body. Like the curled ice and brownstone that he would photograph the next morning.

At dusk he got up. 'Now – it's got to be now,' he said. 'Make a move, baby.' He put on a dub track and turned it up full blast, *likking* the walls of the cottage with ghostly wails and Echoplexed screams.

You dressed and followed him outside where he set up lights on the shore, below the frozen moon. Dub music and waves became towers of sound falling into the limestone mist. His outline, in his bloated black jacket, receded further and further. You watched as he focused his camera on a large black cormorant that was on a rock. The bird was still as a statue, staring out like a messenger from another world.

When he had exhausted himself he lay down on the shore. The music had stopped and all that could be heard was the sound of bubbles draining from the bottlehead bay.

You returned home, and in the months that followed he shut himself away in the study day and night: lost in digital time, manipulating his images of sea-birds, sand patterns, rock formations and blue, frosted seaweed. An obeah man, unpicking the secret designs of nature until flower, bird, rock, water, became abstracts.

He made them disappear.

You shift in your seat and turn towards the bedroom door. No, he is not there. The lights are on in the hallway, but it is an unreal light, cast from the thick, unrelenting darkness of earth moving its way up; the smell of damp just below the surface.

You scroll through his emails, knowing what he has

donc, but not understanding why he has timed these messages to be sent to you after his death. Why is he haunting you this way?

His body had been found washed up on the Isle of Rona four months ago, battered by sea and rock into something unrecognisable – a piece of twisted driftwood.

He must have programmed the emails to be sent after his death; how else can you explain messages from a dead man? But with the rational thoughts come the profane caress along your spine: there are other possibilities.

'I'm skanking the shadows, baby,' his email says. You can hear his voice, low in his throat, deep and bassy. You can see his face, the blood drained away by the electromagnetic blues and reds of his computer, the rake of flesh around the squinting green eyes and the concentrated flare of his nostrils.

'Why are you doing this to me?' you cry out to the empty room.

The computer sets up a shallow soughing.

You put on one of his records, to drown out the image of his bloated body floating in the sea. Dub music: drumming, chanting, deep-down bass, guitars riffing. Horns blowing like a faraway tide.

In the morning you open the door to a damp-haired young Asian man who smells of hair-oil and oranges. He has an apologetic look and a battered back-pack. You explain what you need and he nods his head like a doctor, then follows you to the study. He inspects the computer with his scrubbed clean hands. 'There are more messages programmed, eleven altogether,' he tells you. 'One a month. Wanna read them?'

'Just delete them – please.'

'I can change your email address as well. He may have programmed messages from other computers, you never know.'

'I don't want to see his messages any more. Just do what you have to.'

You pay him in cash and at the door he hands you his card, secures his back-pack and walks away.

When he has gone you take another sleeping pill, one more than you need. You lie down on your bed and close your eyes.

Something wakes you in the middle of the night – a noise, a touch, a movement? The neon light of the digital clock is flashing 3:00am.

You walk, very slowly, downstairs into the study. The smell of damp in the room is stronger now, like something decaying. Two green-light eyes flashing on the laptop. You press a shaking finger on to the switch and the universe of black flickers and expands on the screen.

He is out there somewhere in the black hole of cyberspace.

You know he is.

You are not sure what you are doing when you log on to your new email address, but there is a message from an unknown sender: xope87xoee@universaldark.com

'I've dissected the darkness. Anything's possible now, baby,' the message says.

You click on the attachment and an image opens up of the cormorant that he had photographed on the Isle of Rona. The cormorant is illuminated in obeah blue as it soars away from the rock into grave-dust darkness.

Cold Snap

Maggie Ling

The removal van's outside again. Six owners, now, in only twenty years. Folks don't seem to stay around for long. Spend all their money doing the place up nice, then bugger off. Well … I say nice. Too many fancy shades for my taste. That dining room's been all the colours of the rainbow. Chocolate brown, first off. Horrible it was. Not creamy Cadbury's Dairy Milk. Real dark Bournville. Nigger brown, we used to call it. But you can't say that now, can you. Though I don't see the harm! Like the friggin' black hole of Calcutta it was in there. Sierra Sunset the folks after that did it. Though it looked for all the world like orange t'me. Took several coats for the next ones to tone it down to Crème Fraiche. *Crème Fraiche!* It was white, for Christ's sake!

Magnolia was about as fancy as you got in my younger days. *If* you painted. I preferred papering. 'Papering over the cracks!' my wife used to say. A cover-up job, she called it. Liv liked slapping on the old emulsion.

'Still, this bamboo print'll do wonders for the dining room,' I said. 'You'll like it! You'll see.' And she did! Didn't even mind her painting the doors that mushy-pea green. Always hated that colour. Told her so, later on. Not then. Then we was happy: a house of our own, looking forward to the future.

This area's gone up in the world now. They're all hoity-toity around here these days. Nobody Does It Themselves. Too much like hard work. They'd rather pay a small fortune so someone else'll pick out colours for them, then begrudge the small amount left for the fellas who do the *real* grafting. *Interior designers!* These are four-bedroom terraced houses, not bloody stately homes! A couple of wallpaper books from the Co-op, a shade card from Woollies, and two hard-working weekends was all we needed.

Leisure time. People expect it nowadays. Yet, when they get it, they're hell-bent on rushing about the place, always having to *go* somewhere. Cars choking up the street: parked nose to tail, day and night. The rare occasions me and Livvie got leisure time, we'd get out the deck-chairs, sit under the old apple tree, and not bloody move. Mind you, I've got more leisure time than I bargained for now, and still can't seem to rest.

The last two – them with the Crème Fraiche dining room – were a rum lot. Poofters. *Gay,* they say now. But it can't be right, can it, doing what they do to one another? Makes me sick to think of it. Course, it's always gone on. Went on in the army in my time. I stayed *well* away from those fellas, believe you me. Shaking hands with a bloke is all I've ever done since I was ten years old. My Dad was 'Sir' and we shook hands from then on. I didn't cry – not even in front of Mum – because if he heard me blubbering there'd be ructions, and mother'd get a piece of his mind for being soft with me. So I kept buttoned up. No more cry-babying. I was a man and that was that.

These last two, *Purves* and *Kurt,* took up all the carpets. Even on the stairs! Floorboards everywhere. Noisy lot, clomping up and down. Though, if I remember rightly, they did put carpet in their bedroom. Heard them talking about getting 'a nice bit of shag pile'. Laughing. I couldn't see the joke. Messy-looking stuff it was. I preferred what they'd ripped up. What went on in that bedroom doesn't bear thinking about. I was glad they only stayed three years. Kept the place spick and span, mind. Heard the new owners remarking on it as they went round with the estate agent, walking down the back garden, looking up at the roof, checking it out.

They got the carpet layers in last week. Well, I say *carpet*, but it doesn't look much like it to me.

Livvie liked choosing the carpets. Wanted the place just so. But what she'd pick wasn't cheap. I'd get riled. 'It's *my* money that has to pay for it, Liv!' I'd say. 'You'll have to like something else, dammit!'

She'd get upset. Liv never liked me raising my voice.

Axminster and Wilton were names you could rely on then. Quality stuff to last a lifetime – or more. Now people's fads and fancies change with the wind. This new family's covered the place in ... *sisal*, I think it's called: dull-looking stuff the colour of old sacks, and hard underfoot, not cosy like a nice bit of wool.

'C'mon, Greg, lay down beside me.' It was after the green Axminster went down in the sitting room. 'Come!' her lovely smooth arm held out, 'Feel how soft it is.'

I knew what she was about, and wasn't having any.

'I prefer our firm mattress upstairs,' I said. 'That'll suit me fine.'

She sighed, got up, and sat in the armchair reading her *Woman and Home* until bedtime.

Can't imagine this new couple getting up to any hanky-panky on that *sisal* stuff. Very uncomfortable that'd be. Mind you, they must've been up to a bit of it; they've got two kiddies, and another on the way. Although she'd got a thick coat wrapped around her, I could see her bump sticking out. Freezing it was. A real cold snap. Still, cold doesn't bother me. It always feels like winter in my aching old bones.

Their two kiddies are a handful. Pretty little things, mind. You should see the clothes they get kitted out in. Dressed up different every other day!

I only ever had two suits all me life. Stayed trim, so they always fitted. Well ... Livvie moved the buttons on the waistbands, just a fraction, when I turned forty. She was good at making do, was Liv. Turning collars. Darning socks. Making things last. For years she never *bought* herself a dress. She'd get a bit of material down the market for five bob, run it up, and in no time be prancing around the room, looking lovely.

I'll never forget when she finished the dress with the big blue roses all over it. She looked a treat. Slim as a reed! A waist I could ring with my two hands – should've done it more often, shouldn't I, Liv. Liv never lost her figure. Though she wouldn't have minded if she had, poor love.

That first time she went up west to the flicks with Grace and Avril (*Dr Zhivago* it was, Liv still crying when she got home) she wore that little skirt she'd made from a bit of fawn-checked wool.

'It's *camel*!' she goes, 'And hound's tooth. Not check.'

'Surely you're not going out in that?' I said. 'It's freezing out there, and it barely covers your behind. You're not one of these hippies. You're a *middle-aged* woman! It's not decent at your age.'

'Oh, Gregory,' she goes, 'for heaven's sake. I'm *thirty-nine*! You're as middle-aged as you want to be. And *I* don't want to be. Anyway, it's the fashion! I've got good legs for a miniskirt and it doesn't take up much material, so that's an extra five bob you can spend on beer!'

Dearest Livvie, marching out the door, looking no older than she did in my favourite photo of her: the one I took on Brighton beach, not long after we married, Liv smiling, all sunshine – though the weather had taken a turn for the worse then, too; she was shivering in that sun-dress she'd made specially. Though you'd never know to look at her. Its big gathered skirt showed off her waist a treat. Wonder where that snap went? It was on the front room mantelpiece for years – after I was fool enough to take it out of me wallet. Wish I could see it again, see my Livvie again.

We never had kiddies, y'see. It just didn't happen, did it. 'You'd lose that waist of yours!' I told her. 'If it's meant to happen, it will.'

Liv wanted us to see somebody, have tests and the like. Sperm counts were mentioned. I blew my top at that.

'There's nothing wrong with *my* manhood, woman! Go yourself, if you must! But I'm not being messed about with down there by some fella in a white coat. We'll leave it to nature and be done with it!' and I buggered off to the pub.

She was asleep when I got back, her eyes still swollen

from crying. I wanted to wake her, tell her how sorry I was, turn the clock back, and make love to her in the way I'd sometimes imagined. Make things right. But something held me back. And she'd left early for work by the time I woke up – with a bleedin' awful hangover.

Liv'd got herself a job, y'see.

'Not much good me hanging around this house waiting to become a mother, is there!' she'd said.

'But we've enough money coming in without *you* working too.' I told her.

'Well, this'll be for *me* then, won't it!' she answered. 'You spend what you like down that pub. Now I'll have something to spend on myself. I might even *buy* myself a dress or two!'

We had a few more goes at it, but, by then, Livvie was already forty, and I don't care what they say, it can't be good for a woman at that age.

'Look Liv,' I said, 'it ain't gonna happen. So let's just forget about it, shall we. Anyway, old girl, it's about time we were frigging *grand*parents, not parents!'

That *really* upset her.

'I am not an "*old girl*"! And we'll *never* be grandparents now, will we!' she said, running upstairs.

I felt helpless, useless, so I went down the pub.

I've got quite fond of these little ones: Tobias and Abigail, they're called. Old-fashioned-sounding names to my ears. But what do I know.

Had an Uncle Tobias. Teetotaller. As quiet as the grave – unless he was preaching about the after-life, like he couldn't wait to get there. This little fella's quite the opposite. Makes a right racket. Only six years old and he's got a record thingy ... *stereo* in his room blasting through the wall.

Got me thinking about the afternoon we buried the old man: that first time Liv 'n' me were alone in the house.

Most of the furniture was too dark for Liv's tastes. *Funereal*, she called it. But there was this record player, with a radio and all. A beautiful thing. Mahogany with cherry-wood marquetry, lovely curving legs. 'Almost as lovely as yours, Liv,' I told her. I found this old 78 of Richard Tauber, and we played it over and over, dancing round and round the darkened room.

'You are my heart's delight, and where you are I want to be / You make my darkness bright, and like a star you shine for me ...' I sang, as we waltzed and waltzed.

'Feels like dancing on his grave,' Liv said.

'Doesn't bother me! So it shouldn't worry you, sweetheart,' I told her. 'He was a miserable old devil, and I'm not sorry he's gone. 'Specially since we won't be forking out rent any more. *Our* house, Liv! A family house!'

'Gregory! You'll be struck down,' she giggled. But I could see she liked me like that. Confident. Slagging off the old man with a smile on my face. Later on ... I dunno ... Just got more like him, I suppose. But that day, after too much sherry, after we danced ourselves silly, I scooped up Liv's neat little body and took her to bed. And it was really lovely: her beautiful olive skin glowing in the early evening light and me thinking how she'd look with more of that smooth skin stretched over the mound of our baby. It felt so nice. Felt like it would come to pass.

I never found the lovemaking lark easy, y'see. Dunno why. I'd watch the great seducers, in the films, on the telly, want to be like them, but always felt . . . awkward, somehow. The tenderness didn't come out of me. In the end I'd just feel relief. Don't know what Livvie felt. Never asked her. And when the babies didn't come that was the end of it.

But that one time, tipsy on cheap funeral sherry, it was just right. I knew it. So did Livvie, I'm sure; she looked so radiant.

Mum and the two kiddies came back yesterday *loaded* with shopping – for the baby, no doubt. Then today a van brings a cot, a pram, *and* a pushchair! You'd think they'd still have the other kiddies' stuff, wouldn't you. Unless this one's *un*expected?

They've done the back room out as a nursery.

I expected blue or pink – as you do. Or a bit of lemon yellow. But no. White! *White?* I ask you. That's no colour for a *baby's* room!

Liv had begun getting the nursery ready for our baby.

I choored her on. But something told me she'd not finish it.

'What about a bit of nursery paper with a nice pattern on it?' I suggested, 'Surely that'd be best!' Thinking, it can't be right, becoming a dad at my age. But, no, Liv wanted sky blue. Blue, she said, was a lovely serene colour.

'I'll put one of those alphabet friezes all around, Greg. Low down, so, when it's big enough, it'll be able to learn all the letters. It'll look lovely. You'll see.'

Never did see, did I. Two days later I come home and find her – where I'd left her that morning: stripping the rosebud paper off the walls – curled up on the floor, the crumpled bit of wallpaper she must've been pulling at when it happened clutched to her empty belly, blood all over the yellow rosebuds, blood dried on her legs, on her face where she'd rubbed her eyes. She'd stopped crying and was staring at the wall, rocking backwards and forwards, singing to the bloody, tattered wallpaper: 'Rock a bye baby on the tree top / When the wind blows the cradle will rock / When the bough breaks the cradle will fall ...'

I cradled her in my arms. Didn't know what to say. It'd been too late for a baby, but seeing her like that ... oh, it don't bear thinking about.

Later, I said, 'It'll be for the best, Liv. It's nature's way of protecting the baby' – she gives me a look – 'of protecting *you*! After all, I want you to live more than I want a baby. You're the most precious thing in the world t'me.'

True enough. Never showed it enough, though, did I. If I could have my life over again.

Afterwards it was as if some of Liv's softness had bled away with the baby. She started going out with Grace and Avril more and more, spending her own money.

'What's it to you? You're always off down that pub of yours!'

I wasn't used to her standing up to me. I didn't like it one bit. If she'd done it before, it'd been in a gentle way. Not like this: mouthing off, while slathering on her lipstick, like some tart.

'Don't tell me that's for Avril and Grace?' I said.

'No!' she goes, putting the finishing touches to her scarlet mouth. 'It's for *me*! And to see if *you* notice the difference.'

'If it's coffee and cakes at the Kardomah, like you say, I don't see why you're bothering with lipstick.'

'Well, *I* know why I'm bothering,' she said, slamming the front door behind her.

It was then I started to wonder. It gnawed away at me every time she went out.

Abigail and Tobias are helping their mum fix up the nursery – or hinder more likely. Mum takes it all in her stride. Fit as a flea, she is! Though she must be pushing forty herself.

Yesterday I heard young Toby (that's what they call the young lad most of the time, 'Tobias' when he's naughty) asking, 'Can we stick the alphabet frieze up now?'

If only Liv could've stuck up that alphabet frieze, how different life would've been.

Does me a power of good to see these little ones alive and kicking about the place. Kiddies would've kept us young. Well, Liv was forever young. But they might've kept the old codger in me at bay.

The new baby arrived last week. Had it at home, she did. In a *water bath*! Don't think my Liv would've gone in for that. But the little shrimp's healthy enough, bellowing through the walls like billy-o. Doesn't bother me none, since I can never sleep. It's a comfort, her bawling away in the night: the sound of new life.

And now this lovely thing's happened. The other day, when at last the sun began to shine, I spy Mr Whotsits putting out the deck-chairs. 'Straight from winter to summer!' he's saying. The shrimp's lying in her pram in the shade of the apple tree – well, I say *apple* tree, though it's not given off any fruit to speak of for donkey's years – and they're all out there, lapping up the old sun, when little Abigail says, 'Let's call her Olivia, Mummy?'

'Wouldn't Daisy or Nancy be prettier?' says Mrs Whotsits.

'No!' little Abigail goes. 'She might grow up to be as pretty as the woman in the photograph if we call her Olivia!'

My heart was in my mouth, I can tell you.

'Olivia St James sounds very grand!' young Toby chips in. 'Doesn't it, Daddy?'

Mr Whotsits agrees and it's signed and sealed, there and then.

Seems young Abigail found my snap of Livvie. And something about the look of Liv made them wonder who she was. So Mrs Whotsits sets about finding out. Discovers old Elsie has lived at number thirty-six since 1938. (She must be ninety-three by now, and hanging on to life by the skin of her false teeth!) But she's not *totally* doolally, because she remembers all about Liv and me.

'It seems,' Mrs Whotsits tells her husband, 'Olivia left Gregory to live with her "*fancy* man" in Yorkshire! According to Elsie, Gregory became a virtual recluse, "got old before his time" and, a few years later, "topped himself!"' All the while Livvie's looking down from the mantelpiece. 'The poor man obviously couldn't live without her.'

'A suicide! That explains the *slightly* strange atmosphere this house has.'

'*Had!* But not now. Not since Olivia's arrived. Now it feels like the perfect family home, to me, and I've no intention of moving for some time!'

'Well!' Mr Whotsits goes, 'Since I've no fancy *woman* to run to, I guess I'd better stick around, too!' and he gives Mrs Whotsits a big romantic kiss – like the ones I should've given you, Livvie.

I remember Liv's cries as I kicked her crumpled body on the hall floor, her lovely rose-patterned dress all black and blue.

'Greg! I *swear* there's no one!'

But I was too far gone.

Y'see, for some time, I'd been wondering if she'd started going out with the girls just to pick up a fella, to get herself pregnant because I wasn't man enough to manage it. That horrible time with the miscarriage and the rosebud wallpaper, well, it started me thinking: why now? Why at forty-one? When we'd been trying since she was twenty-eight. Then, after she starts going out with the girls, it happens. It didn't add up. But I kept tight-lipped, let it build up inside me, like I always did.

Liv'd come back late from her date with Grace and Avril. I'd downed a few more pints than usual, and, I don't know what it was? The way she looked? The way she walked in the door? Forty-seven, but young-looking. Glowing. A special glow? For someone else? How could it be for me? I didn't deserve her to love me. And something inside me just snapped. Can't say more than that. Can't remember more than that. Except afterwards, clutching her warm body close to mine, tears streaming down my face for the first time in forty bloody years, holding her tenderly, like I always should've, rocking my beautiful Livvie back and forth, crying, '*Liv! Liv! Speak to me, Liv!*' Looking down at her beautiful, blood-spattered face and thinking: she's always glowed like that, you stupid bugger. Every bloody day of our married life she's glowed like that for you!

I bathed her beautiful body and dressed her in the yellow-striped sun-dress from the snap – it fitted like a glove – and laid her to rest, that night, under the old apple tree. Liv loved that spot. I'd been digging over the veg patch nearby and, with next door away on their holidays, no one noticed any different. Except every day since I've sat under that old tree and talked to my Liv.

I thought folks might wonder. Might notice something was up. In a way I hoped they would find me out. But since I'd said Liv'd run off and left me, was so low, and never bucked up, I suppose they believed me.

I considered walking into the police station. But, then, thinking what that'd mean: being locked away, *not* being able to sit with Liv, and knowing what they'd do to my Livvie; dig her up, take off her pretty sun-dress, cut her lovely body to find out what I'd done. Well, I couldn't let that happen, could I. So I carried on. Kept going, day after miserable day.

I wanted to stay alive so I could talk to Liv, could tell her how sorry I was for what I'd done, could say all the lovely things I should've said to her for the rest of my living days, but I was so lonely without her I couldn't bear it any longer. I'd been saving up the sleeping pills the doctor'd been giving me; those, a bottle of paracetamols, and some whiskey would see me off, I reckoned. Eleven at night, it was, exactly five years after Livvie passed on.

Like a fool, I thought I might join my love. Liv being such a good soul, I was certain she'd gone to a better place. But the Lord's seen fit to keep me here ever since, finding no rest. No complaints, mind! I can talk to Liv each day, tell her how much I love her, ask her, and the Lord, for forgiveness.

It's lovely out here with the kiddies playing around me, the summer in full swing. Most days little Olivia's beside me in her pram, sometimes crying her eyes out. I describe her to Livvie in every detail, rocking the pram, *sssh*-ing the little shrimp back to sleep.

The other day little Abigail calls out: 'Mummy! *Look!* Olivia's rocking *herself* to sleep!'

I soon stopped.

'Don't be silly, darling,' Mrs Whotsits goes. 'She *can't* be! You're imagining things.'

Yesterday I swear I felt a balmy August breeze warming my cold old bones and wondered if my sweet darling's forgiven me at last – or else, him upstairs.

Now, as I lie touching the ground where she rests, listening to the little shrimp gurgling away in her white nursery with the alphabet frieze all around, as I lay my tired head above Liv's, put my hand where her hand lies, inside I feel such a stillness. Maybe I might get a bit of rest at last. Sounds like little Olivia's nodded off. Perhaps we'll all have some peace in this house now.

Car

Naomi Alderman

It's 2.30am when you leave the party. You wouldn't usually have stayed so late but the company was excellent,
the food enticing, the wine superb. You're not drunk;
you're careful about such things, especially when driving. You had one small glass, early on, and despite the
alluring tinkle of crystal and booming pop of corks, you
left it at that.

But for some reason you can't find your car. You had
to park on a side road and you're not familiar with this
part of town. It's made up of narrow winding streets,
lined with parked cars and tiny picturesque cottages.
They're probably astonishingly expensive, you think,
as you turn another corner where you're sure this time,
totally sure, you must have parked. Your car's not
there.

You keep walking, looping back towards where you started. If you really can't find it, you'll have to beg your friends to let you stay the night, look again in the morning or report it stolen. Then a thought occurs. You pull out your keys and press the fob. Sure enough, from just around the corner, you hear the reassuring double blip of your car unlocking. You do it again, walking faster, then once more, then again turning the corner.

But it's not your car. You press the fob again. The car in front of you unlocks. It's a long, sleek, black vehicle – German-looking although you don't recognise the make. The windows are dark. It's low-slung to the ground. Its wheel-rims are black. The street lights barely seem to illuminate it at all. Mounted at the front of the bonnet is a small silver figure of a leaping wolf. You press the fob again. It locks. You glide your fingers along the black trim at the edge of the roof.

You think it through logically. You've read somewhere that the chances of the same infra-red key unlocking two different cars is about thirty million to one. Nonetheless, it must happen sometimes. Perhaps, earlier in the evening, the owner of this beautiful sleek black car found that their key unlocked yours too. Perhaps they stood there, amused, staring at the empty crisp packet in the driver's side pocket and the dirty carpet and decided to slum it for an evening. Perhaps they were tired, suddenly, of their wealth and success, wanted to remember what it had been like when they were young and their mother drove them to school in a car like yours.

You could go back to your friends, file a report on your missing car, stay up until probably four or five in the morning trying to sort everything out. Or you could drive home now in this fluid-lined beast, get a good night's sleep and deal with it fresh in the morning. You stand on the street for a few moments thinking and then you unlock the car, open the door and get in.

You turn on the engine. Is it a little improbable that your key would turn it on as well as opening it? Possibly, but you do not think about this until a great deal later; you're grateful to be able to get home easily. You're not drunk, but you are tired, you should remember that.

The car roars into life, settling down to a thrumming purr. The crisply-designed display glows warm orange behind the polished-to-invisibility glass. The seats are soft black leather. The car smells now. There is less than a thousand miles on the clock. You let out a little sigh of pleasure.

You find that the controls are all where you expect them to be. You're glad to see this car has built-in satnav. You had a lot of trouble finding your friends' house in the first place; the one-way system seemed to lead constantly away from it. You'd been a bit worried about how you'd get back. You turn on the device and programme in your address. It predicts that the journey will take thirty-five minutes. You're relieved – it took you almost an hour to get here. You flick the indicator down – the thick snapping sound it makes is delicious – and pull away.

For a while, it's all you can do not to keep admiring the car's features as you drive. You wish it were daytime so you could appreciate the styling properly. The steering wheel under your hands is both soft and firm, like the welcoming handshake of a new and lucrative business partner. The satnav too is mellifluous, its inky velvet voice instructing you to 'turn left', 'bear right', 'in three hundred metres, take the motorway'. You're not familiar with the route it's taking you, but if it's going to be quicker that's all to the good.

You take your eyes off the empty road momentarily to turn on the radio. A voice speaking in a language unfamiliar to you fills the car, the sound system so perfectly attuned that it sounds as if she's sitting right behind you and you almost look back in surprise. You flick through the presets. All different languages, none that you speak fluently, although you linger for a moment over one of the more familiar tongues, hoping to pick up a word or two. At last, after another couple of turns directed by the satnav you manually tune the radio to your favourite station and relax.

You've been driving for about fifteen minutes now, but you don't recognise anything around you. The satnav is probably taking you a route perfectly calibrated to minimise your journey time, avoiding traffic, road-works, maybe even stop lights. You haven't hit a red since you started driving, you recall. Astonishing what they can do nowadays. You reflect, amusing yourself, that a car like this might even have special roads which normal people like you don't get to use.

You drive on. The lights of the town are to your right, but they seem farther away than you'd have expected. You're on an empty road stretching out across open country. It's lined with elm trees, each with that distinctive leaf-shape silhouette, rustling in the breeze. You glance at the few scattered buildings by the side of the road as you pass, trying to work out where you are. There's a children's playground, empty of course. There's a house with dark windows. As you drive past you think you see a face observing you from an upstairs floor, but you were probably mistaken.

Only ten minutes to go until you get there, says the satnav. But you really don't recognise anything. This can't be right. Perhaps there are two roads with the same name, and it's taking you to the wrong one. You drive on, following the instructions almost mechanically; you'll see where it's taking you, but stop at a petrol station and ask where you are, buy an *A-Z*, get home. How irritating.

But there's no petrol station. You drive on and on, along what look like main roads, but there are no shops along them, no lighted windows even. Only the occasional dark house. At least the tank is full of petrol, you notice, unable to help admiring the curved dial of the petrol indicator. If necessary, you'll drive on. You'll eventually find something open, or some signs. Thinking about it, it's been a long time since you last saw a sign. Probably not since you were quite near your friends' house.

It occurs to you that since you put in an address, a street and house number, there must be houses wherever you're going. It's probably a good idea to carry on.

The satnav instructs you to turn off from the main road down a single-lane track. The road is well maintained but, with the trees bowed over it, and no houses on either side, it doesn't look like you'll find a petrol station up there. You pause on the main road, your indicator flashing. No other vehicle around to be irritated by your vacillation. What to do?

You try to reprogramme the satnav, pressing its glossy screen with your fingers, but it doesn't seem to be responding. Every time you press, it just says 'in five hundred metres, you have reached your destination'. Fine. If you have to drive down there to get it to cancel this journey and start again, so be it. You turn the steering wheel and proceed down the track. You notice, as you pass, that the road has no name sign and feel, frankly, irritated.

The road is narrow and the car is wide. As you drive, long fingers of tree branches seem to reach out and fumble at the doors. For no clear reason, without thinking about it too hard, wondering at the same time why you didn't do so earlier, you lock the car doors from the inside. You drive slowly, with the headlights on full beam. You think you catch sight of a loping animal crossing the road ahead of you – like a fox, but lower to the ground, more like a badger but much bigger – but it's gone in an instant. You wish it were light. It won't be light for hours. You want to turn on the car's internal lights but think to yourself: 'no, then they'll be able to see inside.' After a moment you realise that there's no one else around. Who would see inside? You take a few deep breaths. You're very tired, after all.

'You have reached your destination,' the velvety-dark voice says, at last. You look around. You really have reached some kind of destination – the road only runs on for another few hundred metres before coming to an end, a line of trees beginning a dense forest.

On your right, the road is lined by forest, but on the left there's a break in the trees. A path runs slightly downhill, through an open gate and across a lawn to a large house, set back from the road. The house has six windows on each floor, and two floors. In one of the upstairs windows, a light is burning. It is the first certain sign of anyone else who's still awake that you've seen since you got into the car. You think about climbing out, walking across the dark lawn and ringing the bell of the old house. That might be sensible. Ask directions, find out where you are, where the satnav has led you wrongly.

But as you reach for the door something in you recoils. It's the thought of the long dark walk across the lawn. With the trees whispering in the wind, bending over to get closer to you. And when you reach the house and ring the bell, what will happen? Someone will answer, you tell yourself. Someone perfectly normal. Your hand moves towards the door handle but stops short, comes back to your lap.

This is ridiculous. You're in a car. The petrol tank is full. The car is obviously well maintained. There's no reason to stay here, in this wooded cul-de-sac, when you could go back to the motorway and drive on. You could drive till dawn if necessary, that can only be another couple of hours from now.

The road is narrow, but you're a skilled driver. You'll be able to turn the car round. Quickly, almost tipping over into panic but not quite, you find reverse gear and start to back round, turning the wheel clockwise so the boot of your car almost touches the trees behind. You find yourself thinking 'don't touch the trees', but you don't know why.

You've made a quarter-turn. You turn the wheel anti-clockwise, and start to move forward a little, so that the car is facing the old house with its single lit upstairs window. You straighten up. The car is at right angles to the little road, its back next to the trees, its front facing the house. You prepare to start backing round. That is when the engine cuts out.

The radio is still working. Your favourite station is still burbling on quite happily. The car's lights are still on, illuminating the stone steps down the embankment to the path across the lawn. But the low throaty rumble of the engine has ceased.

Instinctively, you turn the key, turning everything off, planning to restart the engine. You hadn't thought that when you turned the key you would be plunged into darkness. For that moment, the only light you can see is the light in the upper window of the house. You think you see other things too. It seems in that moment that there is something on the lawn, something creeping slowly across it, illuminated only by the light from the window. You think you hear something moving in the woods behind you. You scrabble for the key, pumping the accelerator to try to bring the engine back to life. The lights turn back on, the radio comes back on, but the engine is dead. You don't want to try turning it off again.

You try to think rationally. You can't stay here all night. The car's battery will run down, and then you will be left in the dark. You reach for your mobile phone but there's no signal, no matter how many different directions you turn it in. But the comforting tiny light of the screen makes you think – that's all you need, more light. Maybe there's a torch in this car. A flood-light, even. A car like this, the owner would surely be prepared for all emergencies.

Using the faint beam of your mobile phone's light,

you sweep across the back seat. There's nothing there. You look in the footwell, as far as you can without getting out of the car. There's a noise from the wood, a low hiss. You crane round, trying to see what's there. You can't see anything unusual. The trees are bending in the wind, reaching towards the car.

You open the glove compartment. Your heart rejoices! There's a torch. You turn it on. Good. It's heavy-duty, with a powerful beam. You heft the thing in your hand. It makes you feel better. You shine the torch into the glove compartment. Is there anything else there? Yes. There's something at the back, wrapped tightly in a piece of soft black fabric. You put your hand into the glove compartment and pull the thing out. You unwrap it. Your heart is beating so loudly in your throat that you can scarcely bear it.

The thing is a hammer. With a flat head and a claw head. You shine the torch on the flat head. There are red splashes, with some hairs stuck to dull metal.

As if your head were being pulled on a string, you turn around to stare at the dark back seat. You swing your torch in wide terrified circles, poking into the corners behind you, then suddenly back to the passenger seat, then back to the seats behind. You cannot make enough light to keep everywhere in view at once. Outside, the wind stirs up the trees and they rustle as if whispering to one another.

The back seat is empty. But you cannot stop staring

back. Behind the back seat, right behind it, is the only place you haven't looked in this car. The boot. Right there.

You do not want to open the boot. You do not want to get out of the car.

You turn back to look at the house. The light on the upper floor is moving. You watch it waver in the upstairs room, moving from side to side, and then pass to the next room, then to the middle windows, where the staircase must be. It is coming downstairs.

There is a soft click from behind you. The boot has swung open.

There is the sound of movement. You can see something moving. You say to yourself it must be the trees. But you know what it is. You have known for a while now. You know what you did.

Something is moving. It has the jerky precision of a marionette. It is climbing out of the boot. You thought no one had ever known the truth. It has been twenty years and you thought you were free. The radio softly fades away. The headlights of the car begin to die. You are holding the torch in your hand and you could turn it towards the back of the car to see what is coming but you cannot.

You turn back, forcing yourself to stare at the old stone mansion. In the house, the light has reached the ground floor.

There is a tap, tap, tap at the window of the car. You do not turn your head.

You sit, staring forward, as the headlights of the car finally fade away. It is dark, and in the darkness things are creeping slowly across the lawn. They are coming for you. The satnav begins to speak. 'Be sure,' it says in its smooth, dark voice, 'be sure your sins will find you out.'

The tapping at the window begins again. You wait. It will not be long.

Author Biographies

Car
Naomi Alderman won third prize in the 2004 Asham Award with her story *Gravity* and went on to win the Orange Award for New Writers with her first novel *Disobedience*, which was later serialised on BBC Radio 4. Also serialised on Radio 4 in 2010 was her second novel *The Lessons*. Naomi was named Sunday Times Young Writer of the Year in 2007 and shortlisted for the 2009 BBC National Short Story Award.

The Courting
Gabriela Blandy has a first class degree in history and an MA with Distinction in creative writing. She has won the Royal Society of Literature V. S. Pritchett Award. In 2007 she co-founded writLOUD, a literary event based in London which showcases established and new writers. She teaches 'writing out loud' for MA students at

several universities. She has had over a dozen stories published, most recently in the *Fish Anthology 2010* and *The New Writer 2011*.

The Real Story

Kate Clanchy has published three collections of poetry and won numerous awards, including Saltire and the Somerset Maugham prizes. In 2008 her memoir, *Antigona and Me*, won the Writers' Guild Award. In 2009 she won the V. S. Pritchett Prize and the BBC National Short Story Award and is currently working on a book of short stories.

Obeah Blue

Jacqueline Crooks is chief executive of a charity that supports families in Westminster. She was born in Jamaica and has Jamaican, Indian and German heritage. She has an MA in Creative and Life Writing from Goldsmiths University.

The Happy Valley

Daphne du Maurier (1907–89) was born in London, the daughter of the famous actor-manager Sir Gerald du Maurier and granddaughter of George du Maurier, the author and artist. A voracious reader, she was from an early age fascinated by imaginary worlds and even created a male alter ego for herself. Educated at home with her sisters and later in Paris, she began writing short stories and articles in 1928, and in 1931 her first novel, *The Loving Spirit*, was published. A biography of her father and three other novels followed, but it was the novel *Rebecca* that launched her into the literary stratosphere and made her one of the most popular authors of her day. In 1932, du Maurier married Major Frederick Browning, with whom she had three children. Besides novels, du Maurier published short stories, plays and biographies. Many of her bestselling novels became award-winning films, and in 1969 du Maurier was herself awarded a DBE. She lived most of her life in Cornwall, the setting for many of her books, and when she died in 1989, Margaret Forster wrote in tribute: 'No other popular writer has so triumphantly defied classification ... She satisfied all the questionable criteria of popular fiction, and yet satisfied too the exacting requirements of "real literature", something very few novelists ever do.'

Company

Elizabeth Iddon lives in Cheshire. Her stories and articles have appeared in various magazines and on radio. She was a finalist in the 2002 Raymond Carver Award and came third in the Fish Short Story Competition in the same year. Her stories have also appeared in several anthologies, including *Northern Stories 7*, *Arc Short Stories* and *The New Writer*. She has entered the

Asham Award twice before and has finally made it to the anthology!

The Traveller

Fiona Law lives outside London with her husband and children and worked for years trying different genres and markets as a writer. She began to get published after turning to fantasy fiction about Wiccan and Pagan-related subjects and the paranormal. She has a passion for ancient history, mythology, folklore and all things Celtic. Her love of Britain's heritage and its picturesque landscapes are reflected in her stories. She is currently working on witchy stories for women.

Cold Snap

Maggie Ling has worked as a fashion designer and illustrator, children's charity worker, children's book illustrator, cartoonist and occasional poet, her work appearing in books, magazines and newspapers. Her cartoon collection, *One Woman's Eye*, was published by Virgin Books. She left London for the Suffolk coast, swapping drawing board for iMac to write fiction. Her stories have since been shortlisted by World Wide Writers and *Mslexia*, longlisted by Cinnamon Press and Fish Publishing, and published in *Unthology 1* (Unthank Books, 2010). Poems have also appeared in *Mslexia* and in *Lines in the Sand: New Writing on War and Peace* (Frances Lincoln).

All Over the Place

Linda McVeigh started writing in 2005. She won the Small Wonder Short Story Festival Slam in 2007 and the Short Fuse Valentine Day Slam in 2008. In autumn 2010 she was awarded first prize in the Creative Tourist Rainy City short story competition. She is currently writing a novel. *All Over the Place* is her first published story.

Sam Brown

Kate Morrison read English Literature at New Hall College, Cambridge (where there are sadly no haunted towers) and lives in Brighton. She has previously worked as a journalist, tutor, press officer and, briefly, as an elf in Santa's grotto. She is writing a novel set in sixteenth-century London. Her favourite ghost stories are *The Turn of the Screw* by Henry James and *O Whistle and I'll Come to You, My Lad* by M. R. James.

Vin Rouge

Caroline Price was born in Middlesex, studied Music in York and London and has worked as a violinist and teacher in Glasgow, London and Kent, where she now lives. She is an active member of the Kent and Sussex Poetry Society and has published three collections of poetry, most recently *Wishbone* (Shoestring Press, 2008). She was also co-editor of *Four Caves of the Heart*, an anthology of women's poetry (Second Light Publications, 2004).

A Rose for Paul

Polly Samson was born in London in 1962 and is the author of two collections of short stories: *Lying in Bed* and *Perfect Lives*, and a novel, *Out of the Picture*, all published by Virago. She has written stories for BBC Radio 4 and various anthologies and has worked in publishing, journalism and as a lyricist. As well as contributing a short story to the Asham anthology, she was one of the judges of this year's award. For more information, visit www.pollysamson.com and follow her on twitter: @Polly Samson.

Pandian Uncle and his Ghosts

Anita Sivakumaran was born in Madras, India and now lives in the UK. She has stories in *Riptide Journal* Volumes 4 and 6, and recently won the Ravenglass Poetry Prize. Her first collection of poems will be published in September 2011 by Ravenglass Press.

On the Turn of the Tide

Jacky Taylor is an arts education specialist working in schools, university and community settings. She has an MA in creative writing from Chichester, where she also lectures in Primary Dance. An active member of the writing group Fiction Forge, she is currently finishing her first novel, writing more stories and flash pieces – one of which was selected for the 2011 anthology *The Best of Everyday Fiction 3*.

Red Branwen

Janet Tchamani was born in Worcestershire and educated at Stourbridge Girls' High School and St Hilda's
College, Oxford. She has worked as a counsellor, a
development worker in West Africa and a teacher in sec-
ondary education. She is now Director of The Red Tent
(Heart of England), a social network for women she
established three years ago in Birmingham. She has
written for the *Birmingham Mail* and for *Pendulum*, the
magazine of MDF: the Bipolar Organisation. Janet lives
in central Birmingham.

The Second of November

Celine West lives by the sea and works in the museums
at University College London. She writes mostly on
trains with a coffee in one hand. She likes the Massif de
Monédières, but can't speak for the ghosts.

Acknowledgements

'Red Branwen' Copyright © Janet Tchamani 2011
'The Real Story' Copyright © Kate Clanchy 2011
'Company' Copyright © Elizabeth Iddon 2011
'The Second of November' Copyright © Celine West 2011
'The Courting' Copyright © Gabriela Blandy 2011
'All Over the Place' Copyright © Linda McVeigh 2011
'The Happy Valley' first published in Great Britain in the *Illustrated London News*, 1932, Copyright © the Chichester Partnership 2011
'Sam Brown' Copyright © Kate Morrison 2011
'Vin Rouge' Copyright © Caroline Price 2011
'The Traveller' Copyright © Fiona Law 2011
'A Rose for Paul' Copyright © Polly Samson 2011
'On the Turn of the Tide' Copyright © Jacky Taylor 2011

Acknowledgements

'Pandian Uncle and his Ghosts' Copyright © Anita Sivakumaran 2011
'Obeah Blue' Copyright © Jacqueline Crooks 2011
'Cold Snap' Copyright © Maggie Ling 2011
'Car' Copyright © Naomi Alderman 2011